REXUS

Side Quest in
THE COMPLETIONIST CHRONICLES
Series
Written by DAKOTA KROUT

TABLE OF CONTENTS

ACKNOWLEDGMENTS

There are many people who have given a huge amount of encouragement to me. An extra special thank you to Steven Willden, Nicholas Schmidt, Samuel Landrie, Justin Williams, Blas Agosto, Andrew Long, Dennis Vanderkerken, William Merrick, Mikeal Moffatt, Brayden Wallach, Tom Pachys, Zachary Meyers, John Grover, and all other Patreons for your support! You make everything I do just *that* much easier.

Thank you to all the people that have had a hand in this. To Aaron Crash, James Hunter, and Jeanette Strode for the original concept and to Valerie Reed for the sketch that resulted in my favorite cover. To Dylan Schnabel and all my beta readers, everything you do helps make this project better and helps me create an awesome story!

Thank you to my wonderful wife, who not only encouraged me to write but joined me in the terrifying leap of self-employment. Now we work harder than we ever have, but I'm so blessed because I get to spend every single day with you and our beautiful daughter.

Lastly, a heartfelt thanks to you, my reader. My next book is only ever able to come out because of your continued support! Cheers to you and Happy New Year!

CHAPTER ONE

Jaxon looked out at the Wolfmen pouring out of the forest and across the no-man's land, careful not to show his glee. The people around him were nervous, unprepared for a battle of this scale to continue as long as it had. Jaxon simply had a different outlook on things than they did; this was hundreds, no, *thousands* of creatures seeking his professional opinion on their skeletal structure! He could easily have told them all that their posture was so poor due to their constant hunching, but they seemed to need more *aggressive* treatment plans than a stern talking to would entail.

As he worked on his new patients with his fists, Jaxon noticed that the people around him had changed what they were shouting about. He had no *idea* why everyone else around him was getting all worked up over a silly little thing like the King taking the field; the monarch was only blocking a small portion of the foes from closing in. "Don't worry, friends! There will still be *plenty* for the rest of us! He can't fight them *all*."

Jaxon punched, poked, and applied acupressure on each of the Wolfmen within arms' reach, just as he had since the start of this unfortunate little conflict.

"Hey! Come back here. We haven't finished!" Jaxon's patient was trying to seek a second opinion from his colleague Bard, but the axe-wielding Skald wasn't paying attention. The Monk was *sure* that the Wolfman was only going to tap Bard on the shoulder and ask him to change the song he was singing, but Jaxon decided to remind the hairy beast that he needed to focus on his *own* physical health first. "*Adjust.*"

The Wolfman Warrior yelped as his back was forcibly straightened, Jaxon's class skill using each 'stack' he had applied on that location to increase the power of the adjustment. "Ah, excellent! Now, Mr. Wolfman, thank you for paying attention properly. If you notice, your posture has improved remarkably! Look how much faster your attacks are moving! Wow! The force you are able to muster behind those blows has increased by almost thirty percent! You should seek regular treatment from me."

The Wolfman attempted to give Jaxon the highest of 'high-fives' in thanks, but he must have forgotten that he was holding a sword. Jaxon stepped out of the way, making sure to maintain a smile so he didn't make the beastman too nervous to schedule an appointment in the near future. "Oh. Oh, dear. It seems someone stabbed my new patient and threw him over the wall. I don't have business cards yet! I'm Jaxon!"

Skill increased: Contortionist's Dodge (Student VI).

Skill increased: Wolfman Skeletal Structure (Apprentice III).

He wasn't sure if he was heard over the din of battle, but viral marketing was 'in' these days. And new skills! How nice! Jaxon did enjoy the feedback the game gave him for doing things in a better way. It was always pleasant to know that his skill in a given field was so easily quantified and measured, even when it was as esoteric a subject as knowledge of skeletons. He decided to check on his skills soon to review their abilities; it was always fun to see what the system credited him with.

Something had changed—what was that? Jaxon's vision was suddenly blocked by a new notification, which informed him that the human King had defeated the Wolfman Warlord. Jaxon was finally able to wave away the screen—for some reason it had seemed to be stuck in place—until it was gone, he had shifted around in a small area, expecting to need to dodge various attacks. "Lot of information in that notification! Well, no time to read through the entirety of the message right now, I got the gist of it. Now, where are... hey! My patients are all fleeing! Not *again!* Come back, Wolfies! There is still so much to learn!"

"Ha, ha!" Bard bellowed a chest-deep laugh. "Ye tell 'em, Jax! That's right, ye big furballs! Come back anytime an' we'll teach ye a good lesson!"

There were cheers around them as Bard shouted, which made Jaxon's smile grow wider. He had just learned that the people around him were so *nice!* Offering to teach people that had been considered racial enemies until this point? Jaxon *knew* people could get over their animosity to each other, and he supposed that it wasn't uncommon for young men to get along better after fighting.

"I've never been prouder of humanity than right... what's that?" Jaxon turned and looked at the field of battle just in time to see a wash of white light and heat rolling toward him.

You have died! Calculating... you lose 1,400 experience! You have lost a character level! Time remaining until respawn... 18 in-game hours or nine real-world hours. Time until respawn has been increased by 50% for being in an active war zone!

Jaxon blinked and found himself in a white room with a bean-bag sitting in the center. "I seem to have died. How unfortunate."

Still, he was pleased that this death was seemingly painless; the majority of his deaths in this game had been quite excruciating. Jaxon had even burned to death once, lasting nearly a full thirty seconds as he tried to get to the exit of the building he had expected to explode. He had hoped for a painless death during his self-sacrifice, but...

"Quickly, quickly! What should I do now? I have a few hours to use, and I'd hate to waste them. Which subject to study? What experiment to run?" Jaxon had no real interest in most of the political goings-on in the game, and it seemed that the camera feeds from his friends were offline, so... perhaps he would review his character information. No, wait! It was very likely that he would gain some experience when he rejoined the game, so Jaxon decided to review his skills instead of looking at his stat sheet. Otherwise, he would not be seeing his most updated characteristics and might feel disheartened. Let's see... what was that command? Ah, yes. "Show full skill sheet."

Acupressure (Expert VII). You have reached a high understanding of the application of pressure to the body. Whether with your hands, knives, or needles, you are able to use this knowledge to either hurt or heal. +1% bonus to the healing and harming effects of acupressure per level. +2% critical damage per skill level when attacking acupressure points.

Adjust (Class skill) (Expert IX). Their bones are wrong! You know it even if they don't. When people have poor posture, they are damaging themselves! You can either correct or exacerbate these issues by striking joints. Each consecutive strike on a joint will add a stack of 'adjust' on that location. The base damage of 'adjust' is 5, and each stack adds damage by 5X, where X=number of stacks.

For example, consuming three stacks will deal 15 points of damage. When using this skill to correct issues, each stack will add only 1 point of damage. Bonuses for adjustment depends on how poorly adjusted the target was as well as how often they have been adjusted. Activating this skill will consume all current stacks. Cost: 100-n stamina, where n=skill level. Extra effect gained at Expert rank: You may now have stacks accruing on any number of targets at the same time, though still only one location per target.

Aerial acrobatics (Beginner I). This is a subskill of 'Jump' and boosts the effectiveness of any mid-air movements. Masters of this skill have been known to remain in the air long enough to cross canyons, and Sages are rumored to be able to walk on clouds. Ease of movement while in the air increases by dexterity+$2n$% until the end of the beginner ranks, where n=skill level.

Cloth Armor Mastery (Beginner V). Bulky, metal armor is not for you, and leather chafes. Cloth armor was the choice for you! Each skill level increases armor rating and stamina regen by 1% when wearing only cloth armor. As a bonus, being naked or wearing just underclothes counts! Lucky you, not so lucky society!

Contortionist's Dodge (Student VI). Are your bones made of rubber, your muscles of elastic? You are moving toward perfecting your physical form, and you have found that not getting hit is an important factor in staying alive. Using this skill, you are able to minimize the chance of any part of your body taking a blow by simply bending that specific portion out of the way. Bending is increased by 1% per skill level.

Human Anatomy (Expert III). Through rigorous schooling and study, you have increased your knowledge of human anatomy. This skill impacts all forms of damage and healing to the human body. All effects increased by 1% per skill level.

Intimidation (Journeyman I). You have learned that the most efficient method of dealing with people is saying exactly what you want. Honesty is key, and people have learned to respect that! This skill allows you to make new friends, gain better prices at shops, and speed up conversation. Sometimes people will even give you money for no particular reason! +2% chance to make a new friend, gain money, and get better prices per skill rank. Caution, sometimes people are afraid of the truth *and will get mad about how friendly you are. They may even call guards to attack you!*

Jump (Beginner IX). You have learned how to effectively use your body to cross distances that remaining firmly on the ground will not allow! Whether you are leaping across a ravine or hopping to get something off the top shelf, you find that you are able to go just a little further. Jump height or length is determined by Strength+n, where n=skill level. Stamina costs for jumping vary but decrease at a rate of .5n%. Test your limits often!

Wolfman Skeletal Structure (Apprentice III). Through rigorous testing, mainly trial and error, you have increased your knowledge of the best placement of bones in Wolfmen. Sometimes they can be ungrateful of your efforts, but your work is important! Ease of adjustments and damage to Wolfman skeletons increased by 1% per skill level.

Jaxon nodded along as he read through his skills. They were all very important to him, and he usually didn't go out of his way to acquire new ones. He had heard people talking about having a huge list of skills, but Jaxon found that these nine were the ones that had the most impact on himself and what he did. Why would the Monk bother to learn a bunch of useless things that he wouldn't use regularly?

He supposed that he could take on a hobby or something but was far more interested in perfecting his craft. Imagine what he could do as a Sage of Adjusting? Or of *acupressure!* Jaxon could heal with a touch, disable with a poke, and contort with a flick!

Feeling better about his life choices so far, Jaxon next decided to skim through a forum he rarely visited. The main reason for his hesitancy was that he found their practices... *distasteful*, but they *were* very thorough. As the video flickered to life, a man with an Australian accent appeared. He was currently dissecting a Wolfman and carefully going through all of its weak points. At least the poor beast was dead this time around; that made it easier to watch.

Jaxon listened in and took notes whenever the man found a nerve cluster, needing that knowledge to properly apply pressure or deal critical hits. The lecture only lasted about an hour before the video ended, so Jaxon sifted through the internet searching for new theories, experimentation, and above all else, any advancement in chiropractic medicine or acupuncture.

As per usual, there was not too much that was new to him. This type of medicine hadn't changed much in the first thousand years of its existence, but it had been refined nicely in the last hundred or so. He must have nodded off during all of his study because the next thing he heard was the sound of the portal to Eternium opening. Jaxon hesitated to enter right away, though he wanted to get back to the world soon. He had been doing well in his studies and had found a few other interesting points that he wouldn't be able to study without internet access.

He typed out a message and sent it to his team leader, Joe. *Staying out of the game for up to a few days, doing some research.*

The response from Joe was nearly instantaneous, not surprising since the game was running twice as fast as the real world. *No problem, I'm out of commission for a while anyway. Learning to regrow limbs.*

"Wow! What an inspiration!" Jaxon resolved to use the next few days to progress to a point where he could do amazing things as well. He went through some forums describing commodity sales and stocks in the game and put in a large order for various supplies and such that he would eventually use to bolster his strength. Jaxon looked into build guides, debunked min-max reports, and various issues that gamers had all run into, resolving to avoid them by learning of them ahead of time.

A few sleep cycles later, Jaxon decided that he was going to start falling behind if he didn't get back into the game and get a move on. Smiling happily, he stood and stalked over to the rift in the air, jumping through without hesitation. It was time to see what had happened to his friends.

CHAPTER TWO

A thought-provoking fact: no matter how Jaxon entered the portal from his respawn room—in this case, a half-twist barrel roll—he always came out upright and walking. He had no idea when the transition happened, so he had been attempting greater feats of acrobatics whenever he died. It was a morbid thought, but his goal was to someday catch the moment of transition after death! Jaxon didn't know what he would do with that information, but he was sure something useful would come from it. Speaking of things coming up, the Monk was nearly knocked off his feet as a wall of text assaulted his senses.

Quest complete: Shatter a People. The Human Nation has prevailed against the Wolfman Tribes! Congratulations to you all but especially to the participants. The top three players who contributed to the overall success of this quest will gain a Noble title and a gift of land. In order of contribution, please congratulate: Joe Anti-Mage, Aten Commander, and BackAttack Beastbane.

Jaxon Legend, while not in the top 10 contributors, you have earned the maximum reward possible for your contribution! Reward: 50,000 Exp and 10,000 gold to your personal account. Play on and do great things!

Jaxon grinned widely as he read the information. He loved his notifications; they were so *nice* to him! Joe had complained a few times that his were either mean or snarky, but Jaxon didn't have that issue. Perhaps he was just less easily offended?

"Oh... oh! *Ugh~h~h~h!*" Jaxon let out a scream—or perhaps a moan—of pleasure as the overdose of euphoria washed over him. He was leveling up and up and *up!* Golden light burst from his body as he was lifted into the air. Jaxon was getting a few disgusted looks, but the majority of people were smiling.

This must be a common occurrence right now, with so many dying right before getting their reward. Thinking about the rush he just felt, Jaxon shook his head wryly. There's no way that wasn't addictive, and even *knowing* that... he was already thinking about what he would need to do to gain a new level as he settled back on the ground. Progression just felt too *dang* good to pass up.

Now that his mind was clear once more, he tried to remember what he gained each level. He wanted to look at his character sheet and be fully excited, not trying to determine the values. As a Monk, Jaxon gained three free characteristic points per three levels or a point per level that Jaxon received access to on the third level, depending on how you looked at it. He was also automatically granted one point of dexterity, strength, and luck every even level. A fairly standard arrangement as far as he could tell.

Ah right, skill points! He nearly forgot to calculate that. Jaxon gained two skill points per level and knew that this was double the norm, so he made sure not to talk about it to other people. For instance, Jaxon knew that Joe would love to have lots of skill points and didn't want to rub it in his face. Now, Jaxon just went from level six to eleven but had already used up the skill points for level seven. That left him with... three characteristic points to assign as well as eight skill points!

Deciding to save the skill points until after he specialized, Jaxon added all three characteristic points to dexterity and opened his character sheet. Oh, *so* pretty!

Name: Jaxon 'Legend' Class: Monk
Profession: Chiropractor

Level: 11 Exp: 76,988 Exp to next level: 1,012

Hit Points: 400/400 (50+(350)) (Base 50 plus 10 points for each point in Constitution, once it has increased above 10.)

Mana: Locked

Mana regen: Locked

Stamina: 530/530 (50+(305)+(175)) (Base 50 plus 5 points for each point in strength and constitution, once each of the stats has increased above 10.)

Characteristic: Raw score (Modifier)

Strength: 71 (2.21)

Dexterity: 94 (2.44)

Constitution: 45 (1.45)

Intelligence: 26 (1.26)

Wisdom: 35 (1.35)

Charisma: 4 (0.04)

Perception: 21 (1.21)

Luck: 42 (1.42)

Karmic Luck: -8

He had to admit his stats were one of his favorite parts of this entire experience. Looking at his newly heightened dexterity, Jaxon went through a few of his standard stretching routines to see how much his body could handle. He twisted his arms into different patterns, turned his body in various angles, and tried to bend backwards and put his head between his legs.

He was getting closer to being able to do it! He bet that by the time he got to one hundred points, he'd be able to twist his body hard enough to make it through his legs. Following these motions consistently was how Jaxon learned

'Contortionist's Dodge', and the Monk began wondering if he would be able to take contortionist as a subclass or job now that he had reached level eleven.

How odd. The smiles that people had been giving him before his stretches had turned a little sour. No, wait, what had he been thinking? They were all happy and clapping for him! "Thank you all! I will be working to help other people become this flexible, and I have multi-day buffs that I can grant you for a reasonable price!"

The Monk was not sure how, but it seemed that he was fairly well known. People even began running off to tell their friends that he was going to be offering buffs! How nice of them! A few were even checking his location over their shoulders as they sprinted away to get more people. "Don't worry! I'll be around; you can *all* come and *give me money* in exchange for adjustments!"

Skill increase: Intimidation (Journeyman II).

Jaxon had no idea why that kept happening. Ah well, at least the skill came with decent benefits. It even said right in the description that it helped him make friends! Speaking of friends, Jaxon decided to go see how everyone else was doing. He skipped along the charred remains of the forest, coughing intermittently at all the smoke still drifting around. He had made the small shrine outside of town his respawn point, even though other people had insisted that the Pathfinder's Hall Joe had created would have been a better idea. It *may* have been smarter during wartime, but Jaxon preferred the forest's calming effects. At least, he *normally* did.

About halfway to the town, the forest was simply *gone*. The trees, or lack thereof, turned a once pleasant view into a sad sight. There were still a few tree stumps burning down into the ground, but in general, the entire area was either charred remains or burnt soil. Too bad, really, it would take a long time before anything grew here. Jaxon thought about the seeds he had collected during his time in the instant dungeon but decided against planting them here. They had... *interesting* effects that Jaxon was looking forward to testing in different circumstances. A positive note arrived on the horizon; he could now see that the town was apparently fine! There was the wall, and the Pathfinder's Hall was still looming over everything.

"Thank goodness!" It took him a few more minutes of travel, but Jaxon arrived at the gate and waited to be checked in. As he stared at the guard and the guard stared back at him, Jaxon made a realization and screamed at the sky in frustration. Why in the *world* had he not simply used the function of the shrine to pop into town? That would have saved him a *quarter hour*, easily! His emotions must have shown on his face—or perhaps it was the scream—because the guard paled and quickly began to speak.

If there was anything Jaxon didn't like about the game, it was that sometimes people's mouth movements and words didn't match perfectly. It reminded him that he was in a game, and this seemed like a strange design flaw to have when everything else was *so* realistic. *"Hi, Jaxon. We missed you! You are looking extra healthy and so flexible!* Why don't you go on in? There is no real reason for me to be guarding this gate, so I won't bother asking any questions."

The guard's words made him happy; it was so *nice* that he noticed how fit Jaxon looked! The Monk hadn't thought that dexterity would have any actual impact on his outward appearance, but it seemed it did! He smiled a professional smile at the guard, feeling bad that he didn't know his name. "Ah, it is nice to see you too! Forgive me, but what is your name?"

"My name is Jay; I'm just here on guard duty. *Jaxon, I have back pain from standing here for over an hour. I'm so sore, and my spine is out of alignment.*" Jay's mouth had stopped moving *well* before his words reached Jaxon, but the issue at hand was more important! Back pain? Spine *out of alignment*? That wouldn't do at all, but it was good that this strange little man was so forthcoming with his health issues! Perhaps *that* was why his mouth was moving so oddly?

"Hello, Jay!" Jaxon moved closer and started doing his finger exercises to limber up. Working while not warmed up was a good way to hurt yourself. "I am going to be selling this service as buffs soon, but as a way of saying sorry for not knowing your name, I suppose I can do a little something for you. Let me help you for free, just this once!"

The guard tried to protest that Jaxon was being too generous, but the Monk really didn't mind at all and told him so with a happy smile. The guard pointed his spear at Jaxon and asked the Monk to hold it for him while he was adjusted. Not having anywhere to put the weapon while he worked, Jaxon let him know there wasn't a need for the guard to release his hold on the polearm! He must have told him this too late, but it wasn't an issue. Jaxon simply stepped to the side as the weapon was pushed toward his stomach and got to work.

Snap! *Snap!* *Snap!* "Adjust!" The guard groaned happily as his posture was corrected, and Jaxon waved off his colorful thanks. Stepping through the gate and looking around, he was a bit confused. Why *was* the guild bothering to guard that gate? Three of the walls that had been surrounding the town were gone! Jaxon supposed the guard had mentioned something to that effect, but he still found it strange. Walking toward the Pathfinder's Hall—since the Monk was betting Joe would be in the only building left standing—Jaxon took a moment to consider his team leader. That young man *really* liked to make huge effects like this oversized building. Jaxon wondered if he was compensating for something? Perhaps he finds his class distasteful... or something along that line?

Not many people were around, certainly none of the villagers that had been placed in the buildings around town for care as they worked through the issues they had gained by becoming monsters and hunting people. Oh dear, they were probably caught in that blast. Too bad. Jaxon wondered if his team was going to lose out on interesting quests because of that. He entered the Hall and was once again impressed by the scope and decoration of the huge building. Between the star-like ceiling and the clear floor, walking through the dark building felt like you were walking through space. A nifty experience indeed, and it made this his favorite building in the entire game.

"Joe, *there* you are! Hmm. You seem to be in distress. Perhaps your outlook on life needs an *adjustment?*" Jaxon tried to inject some humor into the scenario for the youngster, but he didn't think Joe understood any of his excellent jokes. Such a *serious* person!

"Hi, Jaxon. I'm glad to see that you're doing okay." Joe took a few deep breaths and nodded in response to Jaxon's statement. "Sorry to say that I am going to be unable to go on any quests for a while. *I'm having an internal crisis. It seems that I have choice paralysis, and I'm just not sure where to go from here.*"

Jaxon stood there pondering for a few moments. Joe not coming along didn't really change too much for his own goals at the moment. Perhaps it would even be beneficial to do some training on his own, or perhaps he could go do quests with the others. Oops, he realized that he might have been standing there staring at Joe without blinking for a bit too long. "I see. Well, I'm sure I can find something to do. Perhaps the others will–"

"Right, the others!" Joe slapped his palm to his head. Strange child. When had that become a thing? Facepalming? Why would you hit yourself? "They were going to join the expedition to the Wolfman lands and finish crushing their society. If you wanted to catch up, there is a second wave of guild members and armies heading out soonish."

Jaxon shook his head in the negative. "I have no interest in tracking down creatures that have lost their protectors. Their society is already dead. I saw the quest reward. It seems a little dark that the game is going to be giving rewards for hunting civilians."

Joe nodded slowly, a look of discomfort appearing on his face. "I agree, but sadly, no one is listening to me on that count. The others are going; the rewards offered were too good for them to pass up."

"That's too bad. I had thought higher of our current team than they seem to deserve at this point." Jaxon tapped a finger against his lips. What to do next? He had a blinking notification that he had been ignoring. Perhaps that would offer some insight.

Quest gained: Finding a specialization! Congratulations on reaching level ten! Now that you are sufficiently powerful as a general character, it is time to progress into a narrower field and become the best at something! What it will be is up to you. Good luck!

Jaxon had been hoping to rank up, and this war had offered a solid increase of levels for him. He turned on his heel and walked away from Joe, who called something about staying out of trouble. Pah! As if he didn't know how to take care of himself. Nothing like that youngster's generation, likely why Joe felt the need to call out advice. Jaxon went over to a small booth in the Hall, sitting in a chair that offered excellent lumbar support and staring at the wall impatiently. A beautiful series of lines began appearing on the wall in front of him, each line representing a path that Jaxon could walk, a way for his class to progress.

Sadly, none of the available options appealed to him: Brawler, Pugilist, various forms of martial art-style classes, non-combat classes... oh look, it mentioned that he could take Joe's class if Jaxon went and talked to the 'ritualist' about it. Huh. For some reason, Jaxon had thought Joe had been keeping his class information under wraps, but right here it was telling him all about how the man is a class trainer. Sighing in light despair, Jaxon stood up and the lovely map of options vanished. All of those paths seemed like a downgrade for him, and he didn't want to settle for moving backwards. Jaxon decided then and there that he would need to blaze his own trail, create his *own* path!

Quest updated: Finding a specialization! You have listened to your heart and are following the true path of a Monk. It may be a lonely road, but self-discovery always is! Optional requirement offered: Find a class and specialize without joining a party. Reward: Variable.

Jaxon didn't need to accept the quest, but it did automatically remove him from his current party. He supposed that was helpful, else he would have automatically failed the quest! Skipping out of the Hall past a few frightened youngsters, Jaxon sang into the open air, "Time to get prepared for a journey! Yipee!"

CHAPTER THREE

Jaxon was standing next to his collapsible table, staring and smiling at the people passing by him. He was hoping to entice them with the powerful buffs he could offer because he really needed to outfit himself with food, drink, and equipment before leaving on his walkabout. If he were *extra* sneaky, he could go to the bank and make a withdrawal, but...

Warrant for your arrest in Ardania. Time remaining: 92:16.

Jaxon grumbled about the false charges brought against him, but at least he could go back to the city in about four days. If those random people hadn't wanted help, why had they *asked* for it? Then! *Then*! To call the *guards* when Jaxon simply requested the payment he was due? Scandalous!

"Excuse me? I see that you are offering buffs. Is that accurate?" An overly muscular Warrior was looming over Jaxon, arms crossed and sporting a dark glare. "I'd like the buff at a discount."

Intimidation ineffectual! Your skill is a full rank higher!

Oh? Mr. Mohawk was trying to become friends with him! Jaxon thought that was sweet, but there was no need for this guy to use a skill; he could just ask! Jaxon smiled cheerfully and began limbering up his hands with his standard exercises.

"Can't offer a discount; the prices are fixed by the national health board! If I offered you a discount, legally, I would need to offer the same discount to anyone who wanted it." Jaxon knew that the laws of his country most likely didn't apply in game, but this random fighter shouldn't. "Armor off, hop on the table!"

The Warrior stared at him a bit longer, and Jaxon got a few more 'failed intimidation' notifications. Finally, the unknown man sighed and took off the bulky armor he was wearing, moving to lie face down on the table. "You're pretty good. First time my skill didn't work."

"No worries there, new friend! I understand very well how useful *intimidation* can be." Oops! Jaxon had forgotten that by saying the skill name aloud, it shifted to an active version. Now this poor Warrior was as stiff as a board. Jaxon quickly decided to offer some free acupuncture as penance. "I can help with this. *Hold still while I stab you.* Whoops, didn't mean to activate the skill again! Ha-ha! I swear, it goes off for just *no* reason at all!"

The Warrior was about to roll off the table, but Jaxon's needles expertly jabbing into his neck and back forcibly relaxed his muscles. Perfect! Now it should be easy to work his adjustments. The Warrior was saying something into the table, but his position precluded Jaxon from understanding what it was. The Chiropractor pulled on the man's arms, pushed on his back, twisted his chin from side to side, then worked over his legs. That should do it for a basic buff package! Jaxon removed the needles, then offered him a glass of water as he sat upright. People tended to be thirsty after a proper adjustment.

"Whoa!" The Warrior took a swing at him! Jaxon took a rapid step backward and prepared to defend himself. "What is going on here? Are you unhappy with the buff you just received?"

"You *son* of..." The furious man trailed off, and his eyes glazed over; obviously, he was looking at the buff. "What in the world? That's... that's *ten percent* higher strength and dexterity!"

"Well, yes, your joints were locked pretty heavily there. I'm unsurprised that you had such a beneficial experience, but

I'd like an apology and additional payment for the unsolicited assault!" Jaxon was off-put by his client's strangely shifting attitude. The Warrior scratched behind his ear, blushed, then handed over the amount Jaxon had requested plus a generous tip. "Thank you for your business! Come again!"

"You know what?" the Warrior muttered while re-equipping his armor. "I think I actually *will* come back."

After that little debacle, Jaxon had a steady stream of people coming to his table. While most of them let loose unflattering insults, they all paid and muttered that they would do it again. What an oddly unappreciative group! As the afternoon wore on toward evening, Jaxon closed down his 'shop'. He had earned enough—he hoped—for everything he would need. Jaxon collapsed his table, folding it over and over again until it fit into his bag. Sometimes it was nice to be reminded that he was in a game world.

No skill increases arrived from his day of work, but that was expected. Jaxon wasn't doing anything new or novel, so why would he be rewarded for doing it? Deciding to make it an early night, he went over to the temporary campsite that his guild had set up, rented a bedroll, and proceeded to sleep soundly through the night.

The following morning, Jaxon awoke to a commotion. The various guilds and the army had formed up and begun marching toward Wolfman territory. Well, shoot. There went the majority of his potential clients. Who else could he offer to help? Jaxon ate a light breakfast and wandered over to the Pathfinder's Hall. Glancing around, he found his next targets. "Look! Over there! Damaged people!"

Jaxon raced over to a group of ragtag individuals that had somehow gotten injured between the war and this morning. Jaxon zeroed in on a man who was whimpering, his arms and legs pointed in directions they should not be. "Hello there, broken man. Would you like me to set those bones for you?"

"Are you a doctor?" The man was in pain, and the wait time to see even a medic here was quite long.

"You know what, I actually *am* a doctor!" This is something Jaxon would never lie about; he could dust off his degree as a chiropractor if he needed to verify it. The Monk was sure he could get it uploaded. "There is a cost associated with this work. Would you like to start right away?"

"Yes, please!" The injured man gasped as his excitement at skipping the line made him jolt his arms accidentally. His legs were in worse condition, though. Had he fallen off a cliff or been wailed on by some monster?

"Done!" Jaxon announced a few minutes later, ignoring the screams of pain resounding through the area. Was it *his* fault there was no available pain medication? "Those should heal straight and proper! If you have a healing potion, I recommend drinking it; that should get you going again! If you don't have one available, I do have a spare that I'll be happy to sell to you for a slight upcharge. I'll need to go get another one, so the premium is justified."

It didn't seem that the man had a potion, and no one else was offering, so Jaxon pulled his out and had him drink it down. Jaxon gave it ten seconds to take effect, then motioned for the man to try moving his arms. "All better? Excellent, the total bill will be–"

"Are you *kidding* me? You just *tortured* me! Why would I *pay* you for that?" The man finished his sentence by screaming, though the Monk was not sure how he managed it. From the abuse this person put his vocal cords through while Jaxon set his bones, he really should have lost his voice by... oh right, the healing potion.

"Well, you did *agree* to pay me. The work is complete, you are healed, so if you *refuse* payment at this point, I will need to undo the work that I have done—including extra for the potion, naturally." Jaxon was sick of people's attitudes! Why *shouldn't* he be paid for healing this man? He would have languished here in pain for *hours* without the Monk's help!

"I... *I*...! Fine!" The man threw a few coins at Jaxon as hard as he could. Thankfully, his arms were still sore, or he may have even hurt the Monk with the rapidly moving metal. This kind of attack was entirely unwarranted and uncalled for, and Jaxon growled a low threat at the man.

Skill increase: Intimidation (Journeyman III).

This skill was silly. It increases for just... no reason at all. Jaxon thanked the man for his patronage and moved down the line. For some reason, the other people were insistent upon waiting for the healers. Perhaps their rates were lower than his?

"*You* there!" Jaxon heard a voice rasp at him.

He turned around to see a guild officer staring at him, several Warriors accompanying them. "Oh? Are officers still around? I thought the guild had mobilized? Are you here for some chiropractic care? I suppose I could give a group discount; that one would be easy enough to explain if needed."

"That is unnecessary! *Maggot*, you are speaking to a guild officer! Atten-*tion*!" The man barked the order gleefully. His expectant look faded after a moment when Jaxon stared at him without moving anything but his fingers. "Ah. Aren't you part of the Wanderer's Guild? This is easier then. Grab him—"

"I'm part of the guild. Why do you ask?" Were they here to give him a medal? They seemed like the kind of people that would put a *lot* of importance on shiny bits of metal.

"Then why aren't you responding properly?" The man's brow furrowed. "What squad are you in? Squad name. *Now.*"

"Oh boy, that's a head scratcher right there. It... name... hmm. I think we are the Special Forces or something similar? I heard us called the Hail-Mary squad by Aten?" The look the man gave him was... *unamused*, to put it lightly. "Does that help at all?"

The Officer's mouth did that strange out-of-sync thing. "*We're going to march you out into the woods and cut you open. If we see you back here before the main forces of the guild are back, we'll keep doing it.* You need to leave the area until Aten is able to return and control you properly."

That was some serious hostility! Jaxon thought 'intimidate' and activated his skill, deciding to use this man's words against him. "You dare threaten *me* in front of a crowd? Who do you think *you* are, *maggot?*"

Swords and various weaponry appeared in the hands of the entire group, and Jaxon knew that they were getting serious. Currently, they were pale and shaking, but to their credit, their weapons were pointed unerringly at him. "Y-you... you'd *better* get out of here!"

"I have business to attend to. I'll be leaving as soon as I've met with a merchant, and outfitted myself for–"

"The merchants are *gone!*" His voice cracked! Jaxon did his best not to laugh at what was apparently a teen playing at being a powerful man.

"Ha! Where's the fire and condescension that was in your voice a few minutes ago, brat?" Jaxon showed some teeth in his smile as the young man figured out what to say next.

"You get out of here, or we're going to–"

"Oh, just stop. You aren't going to do *anything* to me. I could walk through all of you without breaking a sweat. What are you, twelve? How are you shaking so badly against a mere human when you had Wolfmen attacking you two days ago?"

Jaxon tried to lock eyes with everyone in the group facing him. "I think you need an *adjustment* to your willpower, and I'm offering my services right here and now. Be better than your base nature! Be strong, and work to bring glory to the guild and yourselves!"

The only response to his words was a firming of faces, a tighter grip on weapons, and a step forward in preparation to attack. Good. They were able to grow in the face of adversity. Even though Jaxon really believed that these people still needed to ask permission to go to the bathroom in real life, at least right now they were acting like adults. "Excellent reactions, it looks like I properly adjusted your attitudes. Guess I'll be off then. See you all in a week or so!"

"As if we'd just *trust* that you'll actually leave." The leader disdainfully snorted at him.

"I am disturbed by your lack of faith," Jaxon rebutted in a deep tone.

"Men, form up. We'll escort this *torturer* out of *our* territory!"

The small unit stepped forward together, responding with a resounding, "Sir!"

CHAPTER FOUR

"While I am thankful for all the assistance in getting out of town so swiftly, I do hope that you aren't going to be trying anything foolish today." Jaxon looked around the grim faces of his guild members, noting that they didn't look like they would be reasonable. Jaxon prepared to fight them... no! He prepared to *destroy* them.

"Men! *Retreat!*" The people backed away from Jaxon, spears still leveled at his heart. When they were a dozen paces away, they turned and marched off. One yelled back to him, "You'd better *stay* gone!"

"Stay gone? Did he mean stay *away*? Why are they so nervous? Is there a monster around here or something?" Jaxon looked around the area with interest. If there was a monster around, it might have a unique bone structure! Maybe he'd take a look around before heading off on his ambiguously phrased quest. Jaxon turned in a circle and tried to pick the best direction. Nothing looked good, so he decided to leave it up to luck. Jaxon spun around, throwing his hand out and pointing as he came to a stop. That way it is!

Jaxon started skipping into the forest, kicking hard to add as much height to his skipping as possible. This burned through three points of stamina per skip but also propelled him a meter and a half each bounce. He'd say that it was more efficient than walking, but sadly, it simply wasn't true. Walking didn't drain stamina; on the other hand, it didn't increase his jump skill at all either. For Jaxon, it was far more important to increase his skills then it was to be conservative about stamina! Not only that, but with over five hundred points of stamina—not to mention his regeneration rate—Jaxon could keep this pace up for *hours*.

Monsters, monsters, monsters. Where would they be hiding in the forest? If this was reality, they would have either run away from the gigantic blast coming from the town the other day or they would have been lured in to face whatever was making the noise. Jaxon had explored this area fairly well with his team, and until they got into Wolfman lands, they had very few issues. Actually, as long as Jaxon didn't see any bears, he did not think there was anything around here that could give him significant trouble. Then again, if his sense of direction was correct, continuing along this path would put him in range of the Wolfman Scouts. Should he turn? Should he take a different route?

Crack!

Oh? Something trying to sneak up on him? Drat... Jaxon's perception was too low to see what was going on in the dense underbrush. It was unfortunate since Jaxon would have to charge into the thorny bushes that lined the road if he wanted to find what was making the noise. That could leave him vulnerable, put him in a bad position, or possibly drop him directly into an ambush. Ah well, no help for it. Jaxon decided he just needed to man up and dive headfirst into trouble. He skipped into the thick brush, leaving the beaten path behind. The quiet sounds that Jaxon had been hearing became far louder as whatever it was... ran away? Well, now Jaxon *needed* to follow.

The Monk trailed the disturbance for a few minutes, the sounds ahead of him becoming more frantic by the second. It was strange that this much noise was being made; Jaxon really thought that something living in the forest would have better stealth capabilities. He was on guard but was still startled by bursting through the underbrush and into a clearing at full skipping speed. He ground to a halt as he noticed a ball of fur sprinting toward a group of... Wolfmen?

"Whoops, it seems I've stumbled into something I shouldn't have." Jaxon prepared to turn and run for help, especially seeing that dozens of claws and a few actual weapons were leveled at him. Snarling words were passed between the leader and...

"Puppies!" Jaxon joyfully called as he flipped around and charged the group, reaching out an excited hand to pet the adorable little ball of floof. Jaxon pulled back his fingers as a massive paw ripped through the air where his appendage was moving. "Now that I think about it... puppies. That... that isn't a thing, is it?"

Jaxon looked around at the different forms, realizing what was actually going on, why it had been so easy to dodge the attack from the defending Wolfman. His face firmed up as he saw the sorry state of those around him. These weren't combatants. If anything, these were refugees running from the armies rolling through their lands. This group was entirely women and children or whatever the proper nomenclature was for their race.

There was tension showing in the faces around him, and they were obviously expecting him to attack. Sad. Jaxon raised his hands, palm up, and they tensed further. Hmm. Perhaps they thought Jaxon was a Mage. How do dogs show that they don't want to fight without showing submission...? Ah yes. Jaxon dropped his hands and raised his chin, showing his bare neck. The group in front of him relaxed incrementally, and Jaxon received a notification.

Skill gained: Wolfman Language (Spoken/body) (1/10). You have learned the bare-bone basics of the Wolfman language! As this is a basic racial language skill, there are only ten levels available, unlike the typical ranking. Skill points cannot be devoted to this skill; it must be increased through study and practice.

Title gained: Linguist. By intuiting the body language of Wolfmen during a chance encounter and not through study, you have learned how to ascertain body language and speech patterns! +20% speed in learning all spoken or body languages.

That was a nice little bonus. It would also help with his profession if Jaxon could see which Wolfmen were showing signs of fatigue or back pain. It would be even *easier* if they could just tell him! Now... it seemed the Wolfmen were edging away from him. Right, Jaxon supposed that he had been standing there smiling and staring at a tribe of noncombatants for almost a full minute. He had been too deeply invested in looking over all of his notifications and thinking about their implications and uses.

Enunciating clearly and loudly, Jaxon stepped away from them, "I am Jaxon! I am so sorry to have scared you! Jaxon go now! You go be safe! Raise many adorable puppies! Bye-bye now!"

There was snarling and vaguely threatening motions, but nothing came after him as Jaxon backed away. He was betting that the Wolfmen were wondering whether to pursue him, perhaps concerned that Jaxon was simply running off to gather reinforcements. Nonetheless, as he walked away, he was left alone. Jaxon soon returned to skipping, crashing through the forest in an attempt to find the beaten path once more. He was definitely lost, though, and paused in his movements to try and get his bearings. As he did so, an arrow slammed into a tree Jaxon should have been passing, sending bark and slivers of wood flying from the impact site.

Luck +1.

Well, that was beneficial at least. Seven more of those and Jaxon would become twice as lucky as a normal person! What was actually concerning to him at this point was not the fact that an arrow hit the tree he should have been passing by; what worried him was that it did not come from the direction of the Wolfman but from deeper in the forest.

An archer popped into existence about ten feet in front of him, holding up his hands. "Whoa, so sorry about that! All I saw was a brown something hopping through the forest! I really thought you were a deer, promise, dude!"

Jaxon looked down at his brown robe, thinking about what the archer was saying. The explanation made sense, so he smiled at the archer, who took a step back after seeing the radiant crescent. "Not an issue, bow-using new friend! Just out for a hunt?"

"Wow, that's... that's *some* smile you have there... friend. No, I'm actually looking for my party. They split off from the various armies after finding some Wolfman tracks in the area. I told them not to bother, but here we are, lost and separated in the woods. They really want the bounty for hunting down the Beastmen." The archer was smiling for real now, but Jaxon could feel his own expression slipping. The puppies!

"I don't suppose you would turn around and leave if I asked you to do so?" Jaxon's voice came out sounding much harsher than he had been hoping for. The Monk was nearly positive that some intimidation must have leaked through because the man frowned and vanished. "Darn my low perception! He could be right in front of me, and I'd never be able to tell! No, no, *no!* This is bad! The puppies!"

Jaxon fretfully pulled at his hair. No real choice here! He turned around and began crashing through the forest as fast as he could move, his extraordinary dexterity allowing him to avoid tree limbs, roots, and catch his balance anytime he should have fallen. Jaxon returned to the Wolfmen in record time, arriving just as first blood was drawn by human adventurers.

CHAPTER FIVE

"*Stop right there!*" Jaxon shouted with all the force he could muster, pumping so much intimidation into his voice that he actually burned through fifty points of stamina. Jaxon had no idea that he could enhance intimidation like that! This required further research! His voice seemed to shake the air itself, and everyone in the local area froze... momentarily.

The armored man standing above a whimpering Wolfman female looked at Jaxon with annoyance written large on his face. "This is *our* bounty, freak! Get out of here before we send you to respawn!"

Jaxon couldn't believe what he was hearing right now. "Are you out of your *minds?* Look around! These are *civilians!* These are *women* and *children!* How can you attack them?"

"Easy, you aim a little lower and don't use as much force! That way you can save your energy for the fighters!" A man twirling knives stepped forward with a laugh, raising his blade. Jaxon darted forward as the dagger stabbed down at a puppy, poking the attacker's elbow three times in quick succession. On the third poke, a small needle extended and retracted from Jaxon's glove. The penetration should have gotten him right in the tendon and funny bone, but from the resounding scream, Jaxon doubted it felt 'funny' at all.

The armored fighter rushed Jaxon with a roar, as did two other members of the group. Mr. Rogue was still clutching his arm but seemed to find that anger was the solution to his problems, so he reached for a throwing dagger. Jaxon countered by activating Adjust before dodging the sword coming his way. Thirty points of damage rocked the Rogue as his elbow twisted, and the dagger he had been preparing to throw instead fell to the ground and stuck into the dirt. Jaxon risked himself for a moment to try and understand the group he was looking at. As far as he could tell, it seemed like this was a fairly standard group: two melee fighters, a Rogue, an archer that was thankfully not here, and what appeared to be a low-leveled Mage. Perhaps some form of combat buffer?

Either way, the tactics for fighting a group like this alone were very clear: don't do it. They were used to working together and protecting their team, so the only way to win this would be to follow the standard practice of taking down the squishies. To get at the Mage-looking fellow, Jaxon needed to get past the Warrior-tank man and what appeared to be a lumberjack. Not sure why he used an axe like that or what merchant was making flannel in this world, but it was a good look. Jaxon wondered if he could find a flannel Monk's robe, and his distraction almost cost him dearly.

A sword point was whistling through the air towards Jaxon's eye, the Warrior behind it obviously expecting an easy kill when Jaxon didn't move as swiftly as he had been. Jaxon leaned back and threw a couple needles at the Warrior, making him sputter and block his face with his hands. He nearly dropped his sword as well, but Jaxon didn't use the opening. Instead, he used the distraction of the Warrior blocking his own sight to slip around and kick him in the back of his knee, at the same time pulling down on the back collar of his breastplate. The Warrior toppled to the ground as Jaxon bent sideways to avoid the swing of an axe.

"Where were you when we were in the stupid instant dungeon?" Jaxon shouted at the lumberjack, spittle flying. "The enemies were *trees*! Lumber men! *Trees*!"

Jaxon's sudden fury made the fighter stumble backward and raise his axe defensively. Exactly as planned. Jaxon ducked and spun, using the motion to arrive in front of the magic man hiding at the back of the group. Three full-force punches into a magical neck, which included an extending needle, ensured that there would not be any spells flying around. As long as the Mage needed to speak to cast, Jaxon should be fine to leave him alone, especially since the angry, stabby person was closing in on him from behind. As a knife came at his spine, Jaxon stepped to the side and let the blade swing past him. Jaxon grabbed the extended arm, twisting and throwing the Rogue over himself to land heavily on the ground.

"Stop!" Why was that voice familiar? Oh, drat. The Archer had arrived. "If you keep attacking, I'll take you down!"

"I wasn't attacking. I was stopping *them* from killing *puppies!*" Jaxon explained with his hands in the air. The humans were getting to their feet in various stages of pain, and magic man was violently coughing up blood. At least he could breathe; Jaxon had been worried that he had crushed the Mage's windpipe.

"Guys...?" The archer's voice wavered a little as he took in the scene: wounded Wolfman females, the cowering puppies, blood dripping down a sword without a wound being visible on Jaxon. "You guys didn't, did you...?"

"Come *on*, man! They're just computer programs. They aren't real! You know what *is* real? The money we get for their bounties!"

"How much?" Jaxon asked seriously, even as the Rogue was 'sneakily' trying to get behind him.

"What?"

"This Warrior doesn't seem to have many points in intelligence." Oops. Jaxon had accidentally said that thought out loud.

"Let me try again. How much money would you get for their bounties?" Jaxon patiently awaited the answer as the group counted the Wolfmen.

"A half silver a head at a minimum," the Warrior said aloud, finishing his slow counting. "This would net us forty silver, easy. Doesn't matter to the quest that more than half are small, a bunch of them have metal earrings so they'd go for more."

"Tell you what." Jaxon fished a gold coin out of his bag. It may have been a blessing in disguise that he hadn't been able to get to the bank. "I'll give you this if you promise to leave them alone."

The group was eying the gold coin but seemed hesitant to accept. Well, that was the carrot, time for the stick. "Or you can fight me again, *then* attack the very large people over there who will be fighting to protect their young. All on the *off chance* of making *half* this amount of money without losing experience."

Jaxon waved the coin around in an attempt to hypnotize them, but no skill popped up so he must have been doing it wrong. The archer spoke for the group, at least Jaxon hoped he did, "We'll take it. Come on, guys. This is stupid. Do you really want to kill *puppies?* Even if they are just virtual? Game or reality, I don't care where you do it, that's some sick stuff."

"Fine, *fine!*" the Warrior grumbled even as the Rogue snarled at this outcome. Jaxon thought the Rogue wanted to stab him just for fun at this point. The armored brute held out his hand for the coin, and it landed in his palm with a *clink*.

"A pleasure doing business with you, gentlemen!" Jaxon called as they gathered together and walked off. The Mage, still coughing, made an entirely unnecessary and overtly rude gesture as they vanished into the foliage.

Well, that was enough of that. Jaxon looked over at the Wolfmen, who were watching him warily as they tended to their damaged member. Jaxon decided to wait until they were up to full capacity before leaving; he'd hate for someone to attack them right now. When everyone was on their feet and the beastly people seemed to be getting ready to start moving again, Jaxon waved, turned, and started walking away. To his surprise, a guttural voice called out to him.

"Wait, human."

CHAPTER SIX

"You speak the human language very well for someone with a flat tongue!" Jaxon complimented the ancient lady walking toward him. He smiled at her, and she bared her teeth at him in return. "You have a lovely smile!"

"A what? Showing your teeth is a sign of aggression. I was returning your threat in kind!" She snarled slightly every time she hit an 'R' with her words.

"I see! With humans, especially me, showing your teeth like this is a sign of friendship and being polite or courteous." Plus, it was fully an unbreakable habit now; it would take years of conditioning for him to change his ways. "What can I help you with?"

She paused for a second, thinking through his words and pondering her own. "I need to thank you for your assistance."

"I was not seeking a reward, thank you. I also doubt that you have anything that would interest me, as I am not overly concerned with possessions and have no real way to transport them in any case. So, thank you, but *no* thank you." As his words left his mouth, the sound of thunder rolled through the area.

The ancient female squinted at him. "I don't think you understand. We *need* to reward you for your help, or we will suffer the outcome that you saved us from. Is that what you want? To have saved us only to leave us to our previous fate?"

"Obviously not... but..." Jaxon hesitated. They had nothing with them that he could see, and Jaxon would feel like he was taking advantage of them if he took *anything*. He may be considered a bad person by some, but this was not a line he felt willing to cross.

"Travel with us for a day," the crone demanded. "Knowledge can be a burden, but it can also be a wonderful reward. You seem to be in need of both, and... possibly in need of direction? I could see that you understood the rudiments of proper speech. I could teach you more, enough not to be attacked at least. Do you have anywhere else you need to be, or is this something that interests you?"

"I am..." Jaxon had nothing else going on, no real quests, and no idea what he should be doing. Being exiled from all the human settlements really narrowed down your options for information gathering. His next words came out slower than he usually preferred, since he liked to exchange knowledge quickly, "I suppose... I can do that."

"Then let's get started." She turned and barked at the others, and they got moving once more. She stared at a very young, very *fluffy* Wolfman, who cowered away. Satisfied that he wouldn't run off again, she turned back to Jaxon. "What is your name?"

"Jaxon," the Monk replied brightly, extending a hand automatically.

She looked at it, then his face, and smacked the proffered hand away. "No. *Bad* Jaxon! Casual touch is reserved for lovers or family members. If you must touch someone, it *must* inflict pain no matter any reasoning you have for doing it."

Jaxon's eyes went wide, and a smile blazed across his face. "Really? *Really?* That is excellent news!"

"You are... a *strange* human. Never before has that been heard, understood, and gladly accepted." The crone growled deep in her throat; perhaps that was their way of saying 'humph'? She's a *curmudgeon*! Perfect, Jaxon knew there was a reason they were getting along so famously. "Now, let's get on to speech patterns and the proper way to hold your body. When you are speaking to someone of a higher caste, you must hunch your shoulders like this and–"

"*No* can do! Lose my perfect form, high shoulders, and straight back just to *speak* to someone?" Jaxon was aghast at this suggestion, especially when they had no one available to fix the long-term issues this caused their society.

She snarled at his interruption, causing a few of the nearby people to jump away. "*Insolent* little whelp! Don't take the advice if you don't want it, but at least learn what I have to teach you! Close your mouth and *listen.*"

This was how Jaxon passed the next full day as they trudged slowly through the forest, avoiding roads, paths, and anything that might be traveled by other humans seeking them. Jaxon slept soundly and without snoring, which was commented on favorably by the others when he woke up. Apparently, the louder you snored, the lower your caste. Jaxon simply shook his head with a grunt; the snoring was *actually* likely due to their terrible posture and snouts. Mix the physical aspect together with the lower castes who need to hunch down extra small, and you get horrendous snoring. At least, that's what Jaxon assumed.

As their time to part approached later that afternoon, Jaxon looked over the final gains from his travel with these surprisingly pleasant people.

Skill increase: Wolfman Language (Spoken/body) (3/10). You have learned the basics of the Wolfman language and can now speak enough common phrases to have your intentions understood.

Not a huge increase, but Jaxon highly doubted that he would have ever been able to intuit the words and postures needed in order to get to this level of understanding. Their time together ran out just as the group was reaching a crossroads. How very fitting. The crone came over to him as Jaxon was speaking to the puppies. He was being very careful not to touch them, no matter how badly he wanted to pet them. They were at about the same level of linguistic skill as he was, which is why Jaxon had been assigned to practice with them for most of the day. The silver-furred female watched for a moment, flicked her ears in a sign of approval, and motioned him over. "I have not been fully honest with you, human."

"Ah. Is this the sudden yet inevitable betrayal? I'm about to be attacked?" Jaxon looked around, but if the enemies were stealthy at all, he already knew he wouldn't stand a chance.

"No, nothing like that." She hesitated and seemed to be casting around for words. "I *did* pay you for services rendered, but I was also using you as an additional guard during our travels. I knew that you wouldn't let anything happen to the litters, no matter what your personal feelings were at the time, and I used that. My debt has grown instead of shrank, but I feel that I have something that can balance the scales."

"I really didn't mind–" Thunder shattered the air again. Sheesh. Why was he not allowed to help? "It's my *choice* to help, game! Don't force rewards on me!" Thunder again, this time slightly more ominous and grumbling.

"*Enough* of that, please!" The crone was looking around frantically. She pulled a medal out of her bag, and it flared silver as she pressed it to his hand. "This is a small token of appreciation and should grant you safe passage through our lands. That is *not* the reward, for as I told you before, knowledge is often much better."

Item gained: Token of Appreciation (Wolfman). By wearing this token, your reputation with Wolfmen will be set to neutral. This will allow you a chance to make a case for survival when they would otherwise attack on sight. After removing this token, any positive gains will be added to your actual reputation.

Re-equipping will reset your reputation to neutral, though any grievances will still be held against you.

"Now, here is the information that I truly hope will be helpful." She took a snuffling breath through her snout before continuing, "In our lands, there is a temple. This temple is dedicated to nothing and no one. It may even be a dungeon, but it has never been proven. If you make it to the temple, a door will be opened for you, and you will have a chance to prove yourself in combat. The further you advance, the greater the reward you will be able to gain, and I have heard of powerful specializations becoming realized within."

"I also have a *warning* for you. While you are within the temple, you must only use skills related to your class, else the rewards will vary wildly. You can also only ever attempt the trial once on your own. If you fail, you *fail.*" She was breathing heavily at this point and needed to sit down. "Anyone is welcome to attempt the temple, but few ever even arrive at the structure. Be safe, and take our thanks with you."

CHAPTER SEVEN

At least they left Jaxon on a path and pointed him in the right direction. It would have been rather difficult to traverse the forest in an unknown area and find where he should have been going. A temple behind enemy lines... this sounded like a song worthy quest! It was also fitting for a Monk to go to a temple to increase in power, and for some reason, Jaxon felt that this was the absolute correct decision. He supposed that the quest had told him to follow his heart, and he thought that was what he was doing. After all, the heart is in the front of the body, and he was constantly moving forward.

Jaxon continued walking along the path, having been told that it would lead him directly to a settlement that would give him directions to the temple. The old crone had told him very specifically to be careful, leading him to believe that there were going to be fun things along this path. Jaxon started walking, then, remembering, he started skipping along the flat and well-traveled trail. He decided that this would be a good time to train his dexterity, and while skipping, he also began to do flips and cartwheels in the air. This was certainly not the fastest way to travel, but after a couple of hours, Jaxon started to see improvements in his form.

Dexterity +1!

"Thank you, game. That is very helpful." He never stopped skipping along as he read the notifications.

Skill increase: Aerial Acrobatics (Beginner II).

Skill increase: Jump (Apprentice 0). Congratulations! You have entered the Apprentice ranks! As a reward for your efforts, damage from falling has been reduced 5%!

"Those are also handy!" His smile only grew as he continued traveling, but sadly, he was not paying attention to where he was going. Did you know that snakes like to sunbathe on trails and flat rocks? *Jaxon* learned that by completing a flip and landing on a snake's head like a certain red-hatted, Italian plumber. He hurriedly cartwheeled away to gain distance.

Hiss! Jaxon seemed to have angered the serpent. This would be an interesting challenge; did snakes have back problems? Jaxon had never run into a similar issue, but he had a great fondness for reptiles and most of all snakes.

"Hi there, little guy!" The snake coiled and reared up, it's head now above his and waving back and forth. "Listen, I'm so sorry about that. I love snakes and would have never intentionally attacked you. You are all *spine*! It's *glorious*!"

He was nearly shouting by the end of his small speech, and the snake had gone still. Its tongue flicked out repeatedly, the only part of it noticeably moving. *Whisk*! Jaxon contorted to the left, dodging the finger-length fangs that had been aiming for his neck. "Oh, come on! My snakey-snake, why are you making me do this? I already said sorry!"

Whisk *Whisk*! Jaxon slid to the right, then tumbled into a somersault to avoid the follow up strike. "I don't want to fight you, and I *won't*"

Quest gained: Betting your life! A Monarch Death's Touch Asp has targeted you for an infraction. Although you apologized, the mean ol' snake just woke up and is grumpy! You promised the snake that you wouldn't fight it, so let's see what happens! Avoid the unbelievably poisonous fangs long enough for the snake to get bored and leave. Failure requirements: Attack the snake or get bit. Reward: 5 points to dexterity, variable. Failure: Death or Warlock title, double Exp penalty.

Jaxon almost faltered as the quest appeared, the fangs brushing the strap of his backpack, corroding it in the same moment. As he cartwheeled over the next attack, the strap broke, and he needed to let the pack fall to the ground. He had gained a few feet of wiggle room, or so he thought. The Asp moved forward in a straight line across the ground, not winding like a normal snake in the slightest. It left a furrow on the ground of smooth, packed dirt, leading Jaxon to believe that it had some kind of earth manipulation ability.

The front of the snake lifted off the ground as it approached, like the prow of a ship that was moving across water extra speedily. Jaxon was off-balance, and the only option was up. As he gained a firm foothold and jumped forward into an aerial somersault, the snake came further off the ground and fangs opened to catch him. Jaxon burned through nearly a hundred points of stamina with his next maneuvers; Contortionist's Dodge was used to his maximum ability, and his ribs shifted up and over the Asp's mouth. The rest of his body slid along the snake, and he rolled down its length as it passed under him.

Jaxon hopped to his feet and stared the snake down as it swung around to face him once more. He started weaving his body side-to-side, arms held out and moving independently in slow arcs. His fingers were also wiggling as he warmed up. Jaxon hoped that blocking an attack wouldn't count as attacking because he was starting to run low on stamina. The Asp, seeing him move like this, coiled up and reared back.

It locked eyes with Jaxon, and its head started moving in time with his own. Jaxon, understanding that something had changed, continued moving in similar patterns. He slowed down incrementally over time, but the snake stopped following his movements well before he got close to stopping or needing to stop. With a somewhat agitated hiss, the Asp slithered away through the underbrush. Jaxon took a deep, calming breath, then screamed as a wall of text and pain slammed into him.

Quest complete: Betting your life! You charmed a Monarch Death's Touch Asp into leaving you alone! While you certainly didn't tame it—a feat believed to be impossible—your movements struck a chord in its snakey little brain. Perhaps it thought that you were another of its kind? Reward: +5 Dexterity, Title: Snake Charmer.

Snake Charmer: You have shown that your love for snakes is true, refusing to fight even on the verge of dying! In the future, it will be 20% easier to tame reptiles, and snakes especially will show you favor, attacking you last if possible.

You have reached a threshold of 100 dexterity! Your nerves, reaction times, and bodily movement ability are being modified; please lie down to avoid falling and hurting yourself! Starting in 2... 1...

Jaxon hadn't even been in this much pain when he had burned to death over thirty seconds. His skin rippled as his muscles were forcibly contracted, and his limbs spastically twitched. His head thrashed side to side, and the only reason he didn't bite his tongue was that his jaw was too firmly clenched. Then Jaxon felt his bones change. This was the most terrifying aspect to him, as he knew exactly what his body could handle to this point. Then the pain and fear went away, and he was left with pure excitement that he once again had the opportunity to explore a new body.

He was flat on his back in the middle of the road, a few cuts from sharp rocks dripping blood. He didn't mind *one bit*, Jaxon only had smiles today. His legs lifted up, then bent to put the pads of his feet flat on the ground. Ever so slowly, Jaxon straightened his body into a standing position without ever needing to use his hands or force to get into that position. "I'm made of rubber! I bet that looked like a scene from a horror movie!"

He was correct, and the one person who had witnessed the event was nearly sick from watching the inhuman motions. A dagger glinted in the light briefly as they considered moving against the target early... no. Jaxon was going to be leading the team to treasure; moving against him now would be foolish. The knife vanished into a sheath, even as the figure vanished into the shadows.

"While that was fun, I seem to be out of stamina. Time for a snack, a rest, and then onward to destiny!" Jaxon folded his legs and plopped down to the ground, landing gently although he wasn't trying to do so. He pulled over his damaged bag, reaching in for some travel rations and a sewing kit. He sewed the strap back to the bag, nodding when he pulled at the ugly work and it held.

Skill gained: Sewing-

"Don't want it," Jaxon loudly spoke even as the rest of the information began appearing. Then he waited with anticipation. This was a trick he had learned, the secret to his amazing success and the only way he knew of to get ahead in the game. This was the *one thing* he would never tell another person.

Are you sure you want to refuse learning the skill [Sewing]? If you refuse this skill, the only way to learn the first rank of skill [Sewing] will be to devote five skill points to learning it. Yes / No.

"Yes, refuse skill," Jaxon subvocalized the words, never knowing who may be listening in.

You have refused the skill [Sewing]! Five free skill points have been added to your sheet!

"Excellent." That put him at thirteen free skill points. Looking at his skills, he finally broke under the pressure and used three points to bring his two most-used skills to the next ranking. Even though he only had ten free points right now, the hope was that it would be enough to be beneficial to any skill he may gain during specialization.

Skill increase: Adjust (Master 0). Congratulations! You have reached mastery of your main class skill! Mastery reward: The base damage of 'adjust' has been doubled! Base damage is now 10, and each stack adds damage by 10X, where X=number of stacks. When healing, the penalty has been halved! Now only 0.5 points of damage are given when adjusting to help others!

Skill increase: Acupressure (Master 0). Congratulations! You have reached mastery of the application of pressure to the body. Mastery reward: Critical damage done to acupressure points has been doubled! Current critical hit bonus: 240%.

It had been a long time coming, but Jaxon was now a Master at his craft! He wanted to shout his glee to the world. Instead, he simply got to his feet and began skipping down the road with renewed vigor. His body moved in perfect sync with itself, and his head remained stable even as the rest of him shifted fluidly. There was a sharp pang as he overdid it; it looked like his constitution wasn't high enough for him to avoid damage when he went just a *little* too far. He almost wanted to pick a fight with something or someone just to see the limits and benefits of his new threshold and skill levels! It seemed that all of the Wolfmen in the area had been mustered for war, however, and Jaxon didn't see a single one of the race's combatants anywhere.

He heard a bugle off to his left, followed by a series of rapid explosions. He must have caught up to where the army was waging their war! Jaxon slowed slightly, then shook his head and picked up the pace. If he left this path, he might never find it again! Specialization needed to come first. Besides, it wasn't as if there was any real benefit for him in the war as it stood. The quest had been completed. Right now, it was a slaughter of a shattered race, and that was just genocide. Jaxon decided to do a few more flips. He was really enjoying the feel of his body! How tightly could he curl himself while in the air? Jaxon never saw the overturned earth or magic flowing in the ground under him; he was far too entranced with his body.

Luck +1!

"I agree, game! Doing flips at my age *is* oddly lucky!" Jaxon happily skipped, twirled, and pirouetted down the path, all the while somehow avoiding pitfalls, explosive traps, and patrols of both the human and Wolfman army. The signs of their passing or setup were obvious to those who knew what they were looking for, but Jaxon was only looking for the next landmark he had been told would be in his path. Hours passed, and he found no enemies, no monsters, and no signs of life whatsoever.

"Jolene, Jolene, Jolene, Jole~e~ne! I'm begging of you, please don't take my life!" Jaxon had started singing to pass the time as he continued onward and was hoping that something interesting would happen as he sang. "All you've ever brought is pain and strife; your teeth are sharp, your mouth takes life; your claws rend flesh, there's no escape... from the judgement of the eldritch one, Jolene!"

Would you like to change class to 'Dark Bard'? Skills include summoning magics, debuffs for friends and allies, and self-sabotage. Yes / No.

"No thank you, game." Jaxon furrowed his brow. "Perhaps I should be more careful of what I'm singing?"

His eyes lit up as the late afternoon heat began shifting to the chill of evening. In the distance, a tribal-style palisade was coming into view, and hulking sentries were watching him approach. Snarls and barking filled the air, warning to others that an invader was approaching. Jaxon clipped on his 'Token of Appreciation' and waved at the gate guards. He shifted to their language, and the nearest winced as he butchered their native tongue.

"Heelloo, fellow fist-punchers! I arrive here to go to Temple of Rewarding Tests! I pass through? You want *chiropractic services*?" The last few words were in English, as the Wolfmen simply didn't have a translation for them. "I give good trade! You strong, me money getting! Democracy and peanut!"

The sentry was confused at a few of the words, but when he saw the token, he nodded and let down a rope. There was no need for gates around the town; only children needed ropes to get in and out, but Jaxon didn't understand the insult and clambered up. "Ah! My grati-thanks! I can close eyes in peace and rest here?"

He smiled around at the Wolfmen who were now surrounding him. What an unexpectedly cordial welcome; they were smiling! Wait. Didn't smiling mean something different to them?

CHAPTER EIGHT

"That man is *insane*." Jessamyn disarmed yet *another* trap in the road, this one basically a landmine that would first shatter the armor of anyone standing on it, then explode. Her progress in tailing him had slowed significantly when she encountered the first trap. Unlike Jaxon, she couldn't safely leap over the majority of them; she needed to carefully search for them and then either avoid or disarm them.

Jess had been following Jaxon ever since he had appeared screaming outside of a shrine. His gear looked really good, and the way everyone ran from him suggested that he had power and money. Why else would they have those looks of fear on their faces? The man had made what *should* have already been a fatal mistake; he was alone. Somehow, though, he kept making the strangest choices! Instead of attacking the Wolfmen, he had *traveled* with them for a day! She had been waiting for the red aura of a racial traitor to appear so she could rob and slay him worry-free, but it never showed up.

All of her carefully laid traps on the paths and roads he would have been using if he had gone back to where he started? Useless! Then... then! The deadly Asp she had lured to the area? It left because the man *annoyed* it away! That had taken *hours* of carefully placing prey and heating a small section of the road for it to digest its food on! That more than anything was causing her a headache. Now, on the deadliest stretch of road trapped by both Humans and Wolfmen, Jaxon had *sped up*. Jess had no idea where he was going, but it was sure to be a place with untold treasures. She had to find him, or when the rest of her team caught up, they would boot her from the party.

She shivered at that thought. She was trying to get into a very exclusive guild that planned on focusing on player-versus-player combat, and on the final mission before becoming a full member, she was *failing*! She had already been loaned a 'Graverobber's Kris', which was the secret weapon of her guild. It allowed her to loot a random item from any player she killed, and she had originally planned to take out the Monk as soon as possible. *Why* had she listened to that stupid... right, the possibility of *real* treasure. She sighed, getting back to work on clearing a small path through the megatons of explosives this road contained.

JAXON

"Hello, big Chief Wolf!" Jaxon smiled winningly at the extra-large Wolfman he had been brought before. Once again, he didn't know the Wolfman word for something, but that wouldn't stop him from trying, "You first *patient*?"

"I'm not a Chief," the Wolfman replied in passable English. "Why are you here? Why should we not slaughter you and give our pups a taste for manflesh?"

Jaxon nodded along at his words. "I see, I see. You have hungry children and need a discount. I don't think there are any rules on discounts for non-human sapients, so I won't tell if you don't. As to why I am here, an old Wolflady sent me this way and told me that you would give me directions to a temple that might help me specialize."

"What if I said I didn't believe you?" The Wolfman's ear twitched back and forth lazily. "What if I said that you killed one of our people and took that token off their corpse?"

"Oh, *right.*" Jaxon snapped his fingers loudly, causing not a few weapons to be pulled from sheaths. "I was supposed to tell you a phrase if this came up... let me think... what was it...? Got it! Let me see if I can pronounce it in wolf-tongue properly. '*You leave this one alone, or I will leave you shaking you like a poodle.*"

The room went silent, and even the socially dense Jaxon noticed. "A-*hem*, yes, but she didn't tell me what it meant, just made me memorize it perfectly."

A strange chuffing sound came from the Wolfman, and Jaxon could have sworn that he saw a tail wag once or twice. The Wolfman was *laughing*? "You met *O'Baba*! My people, O'Baba *lives!*"

There was a moment of quiet, and then whispering broke out, what passed for whispers among their people anyway. "You bring us joyous news! But tell me, *fist-puncher*, why would O'Baba vouch for you?"

"Now, first off, I am uncertain if that was her name." Jaxon held up his gloved hand to make sure that fact was known. "I was given this token after rescuing a pack of Wolfladies and puppies... err... I don't know what you call children here. Then the elderly Wolflady made me travel with them for a day to learn some of your throat-damaging, guttural language."

For some reason, his words were laughed at, and chuffing erupted in the area. "You... you *saved* O'Baba? Was the human King or Queen attacking her? *What* did you save The People's *most powerful* shaman from?"

"She was being attacked by a group of humans that had bounties for kills." Jaxon's words brought another round of chuffing. "Even if she is as powerful as you say, since she was protecting others... I think the real reason I was given this token is that no one else got killed."

The laughing stopped, and the Wolfmen shifted slightly on their feet, wanting nothing more than to have this human stop making them uncomfortable. His words made them realize that it was *possible* that a few pups may have been slain if he hadn't intervened. Not-the-Chief huffed through his snout and spread his arms wide. "If the O'Baba gave you her personal token, who am *I* to refuse you? Now, you wanted to trade? What can you offer?"

"Offer?" Jaxon's eyes lit up, and he needed to wipe a line of drool off his chin. For some reason, he couldn't contain his excitement at being able to help a new race adjust. "Yes! I can *adjust* your bodies, allowing you to move correctly and be more powerful. While it is not a permanent effect initially, over the course of several sessions, your body will become far stronger! I can use myself as an example."

Jaxon twisted around in a dizzying whirl; bending, twisting, and flipping to show his flexibility and strength. He was holding himself up with a single finger when the Wolfman stopped him, speaking with out of sync mouth movements, "Please, yes, you can stop. There is *nothing I would like more than this buff you offer.*"

"Then have it you shall!" Jaxon stepped forward and started driving his fingers into the various acupressure points he had been able to discover or learn about.

The third poke sent a needle into a nerve cluster, forcing the Wolfman to choke back his cry of rage at the sudden but somewhat expected assault. His eyes went wide as the human grasped his head and *twisted*, sure that this was the end for him. Instead, there was a *pop*, and his head was twisted another direction. *Pop*. The expected pain never arrived. Instead, relief began to flow through him. The human was suddenly on his back, grasping the armor on his shoulders and pressing down with his feet while leaning backward. *Crack*!

"Hyperkyphosis. Tsk, tsk. Your caste system is seriously impeding your body's natural ability to stand erect." Jaxon hopped down to the ground and stepped back. Wiping his hands off, he smiled as the Wolfman began moving again. The huge beast took a step forward and stood straight, the slouch he had always walked with removed for the first time in his life. He was suddenly standing over a foot taller, and his presence washed over the others like a physical blow. They averted their eyes and slouched lower; obviously, their leader had somehow just become an actual chief!

"I feel... amazing. You could have killed me, yet you didn't..." The Wolfman growled deeply and moved with higher agility than he had ever been able to manage. "You also followed our rules, ensuring to inflict some pain with each touch so that my constitution could improve over time. This buff...! No! It lasts *how* long?"

Feat of honor performed! Your reputation with the Wolfmen has increased by 800! Current reputation is: 0 (forced neutral). Actual reputation is: -2200 (Hated).

"Should be about three days, but repeated usage increases the length." Jaxon happily smiled as the Wolfmen around him began to murmur and shift closer. They had planned to attack him, but at their new Chieftain's words, they instead began vying for a closer position. His next words barely even gave them pause. "Now, Mr. Wolf, what would you say is a fair price for this treatment?"

CHAPTER NINE

"Skipping *freak*, vanishing along a road that I barely survived *cautiously* moving along!" Jess was covered in mud, blood, and her armor was scorched and charred from failed attempts to disarm traps. It had also just started to rain. Today was not her idea of fun times. "When I catch up to him, I don't care what the others want; it's stabbing time! I'll get into the guild, get the recognition I deserve, and make giant barrels of money. Then-*gah!*"

Jess stopped short just as a sword whistled through the area her head should have been. She had forgotten to go into stealth and was now staring at a small pack of Wolfmen as they surrounded her. She screamed her frustration as she was forced to dodge another attack. "Well isn't this just *perfect!* You *suck!*"

The world went dark for her as she was clubbed over the head from behind, and she found herself standing in her respawn room looking at a notification. When she finished reading it, she screamed in frustration.

You are unconscious! Warning: you are currently a prisoner of war!

In Eternium, a Wolfman had lifted her comatose body and carelessly tossed her over his shoulder. They started walking toward town in a good mood; they had a prisoner! One of three things would happen next. They would slay her before she awoke and use her body for various crafting components and food, give her to a Shaman, or... perhaps the strange human would trade some of his power-pain buffs for her life. At their loping speed, the pack reached town and brought the prisoner over to the small area the human had set up. He was surrounded by smoked meats, cured hides, and various other commodities that were either of low value to the wolves or something that they could go without.

"Step up right, wolf-friends!" Jaxon called in a terrible rendition of their proper tongue. "Strong making power-pain! Small cost, large gain!"

"We need to get you some more practice with our speech," the leading Warrior jeered at Jaxon. The man in question simply stared back at him blankly, his artificial smile causing their hackles to rise.

"Thank you for interest, but words too big to catch. You want trade?" Jaxon was speaking slowly but still failing spectacularly at their tongue.

"I have woman!" the Wolfman Warrior called out in equally broken English. "I give to you, whole party gets pain-power!"

"Pain-power, that's a cute name for Chiropractic care." Jaxon chuckled lightly, obviously not understanding that he had been saying something similar. He looked at the lady in question, getting a nagging feeling that he had seen her before. Jaxon responded in their language, trying to haggle—badly, "Whew! Stinky! She worth *whole* friends getting pain-power?"

"Up to you." The Wolfman flicked his ears, their version of shrugging. "Either that or we eat her and pay another way."

Jaxon hesitated, then looked at the stack of goods he had collected. He looked back at the lady, then the goods, and shrugged helplessly. "I... suppose. Please get in line and lay on the table, there is far more I can do for your bodies on a proper surface."

The Wolfmen chuffed, knowing they had gotten a good deal out of him. It was *very* likely that someone would cut down the female human when she was up and moving around again. It was unlikely that she had been coming toward them with good

intentions, and the second she acted out or left Jaxon's side...
someone would pounce. Jaxon went fairly quickly with these
adjustments; knowing that he was being taken advantage of
made him work more *forcefully* than usual. Yipping and whining
were common as he used his glove's needles less *accurately* than
he could have. Still, the Wolfmen were pleased by the outcome
of their deal and left standing taller and straighter.

Jaxon glared at the still form of what he assumed was an
assassin type, cracking his knuckles. She would need to pay him
back for the rescue and the free care he had needed to give the
Wolfmen. He sat down on his table, having no patients waiting,
and stared at her as the rain started to pick up. He was under a
lean-to and staying dry, but she was flopped awkwardly on the
ground in a slowly growing puddle. Jaxon watched with interest
as she regained consciousness. The process was very different in
this world. Instead of slowly coming around and being confused,
her eyes popped open and she hopped to her feet ready to fight.
Jaxon saw her wince as what must be a horrible headache
arrived.

"Good *morning*, Sunshine!" Jaxon called to her with a
wide smile. He wanted to be friendly with her, but he had really
needed the supplies he would have been getting from the
Wolfmen. Jaxon had heard a few rumors about the trip that was
making him want to be extra cautious, and bringing enough to
satisfy his basic needs would be hard to do if he had to keep
giving out freebies. All of this added up to him being a *tish* upset
that she had been captured. "So... I kept the Wolfmen from
eating you while you were asleep, but it cost me quite a bit. I am
going to need you to reimburse me."

Jess reached for her dagger, determined to end this fool
even if it took a head-on fight. Her palm slapped against her
pants, and she went pale instantly. It was *gone*! Her

Graverobber's Kris! She couldn't loot his body without it and losing it was enough to lose her chance at admittance to the guild no matter what she did. "*Mother-*"

"Hey! Please keep your voice down. You don't want to... this should be good." Jaxon shifted around on his seat as the lady turned and ran away from him. She got eight feet away before a Warrior appeared out of the rain and loomed over her. It slapped her in the chest at full force with a snarl, sending her tumbling back *almost* to her starting position, this time gasping for air and bleeding. "I may not have had a chance to mention that we are in a Wolfman stronghold. The only reason you are alive is that I bartered for your life. Now, according to your health bar, if you want to go back to your spawn point, you can try that again. Otherwise, you are going to have to leave with me and find a way back to the humans."

"Leave *with* you?" Jess suddenly had hope in her eyes; maybe she could convince him to take her willingly to wherever he was going. If she was able to secure a treasure trove, perhaps the guild would be forgiving about the loss of the dagger. It wasn't like a rival guild had the weapon; it had been stolen by a Wolfman! "Sorry I tried to run, I freaked out a little. I'm Jess. Thank you for saving me."

"Well! Proper manners!" Jaxon clapped lightly as his eyes lit up. "Wonderful, I had been thinking that no one remembered that 'please' and 'thank you' were words still in circulation! They play a game and become unaccountably rude for no reason other than it 'isn't real'. You are very welcome, and... perhaps I was a bit hasty in demanding payment. Payment probably shouldn't be required *not* to be eaten. That should be *normal*, right? Right."

Jess started thinking that she had made a huge mistake. Her group had been chasing him because they thought this man had wealth and influence, but up close, it was easy to see that his gear was at low durability and he was just strange and *intimidating*. It was likely that people hadn't been avoiding him for fear of his social power; they had just been avoiding *interacting* with him! She put her face in her hands. "I know I don't seem to have much choice, so I'd be happy to wait. But, if you don't mind my asking, where are you going?"

She was expecting the worst, so his next words made her perk up in abject glee. "Going? Oh. I'm going to a temple that gives out amazing rewards for clearing challenges. I'm not sure if it will be super rare items, skills, classes, or just a river of gold, but it's only a few days away."

"Are you messing with me?" She looked at his face, which only showed uncertain confusion alongside his creepily ever-present smile. It was like looking at a skeleton.

"Why would I do that?"

Jess broke into a brilliant smile. "Is there any way that I could work off my debt to you? Perhaps you need a travel companion to help keep watch at night?"

"I'm not really into that sort of thing, thanks. I prefer to date and such. I'm not a person who pays for company and working it off isn't..." Jaxon smiled at her apologetically, but as her face turned red, he finally dropped his smile and appeared startled. "Oh! I apologize! You mean like moving along as a *party*? I can't do that, sorry. I'm on a solitary quest and adding anyone to my party will cause me to fail it."

"*Ahem.*" Jess cleared her throat and tried again. She *needed* him to take her along! "If we are just traveling to the same place, not in a party, is that acceptable?"

"*No,*" Jaxon snapped at her, eyes full of fury. She reeled back, and Jaxon coughed into his hand. "No, I don't see any reason that wouldn't work. Sure, let's be travel buddies!"

"U-um. Okay then?" Jess wasn't sure what to say; what would set off the freaky man, and what would be fine? She had to play it safe. If he discovered that she planned to rob him, it would be difficult to escape from the area. Perhaps flattery was the best option to throw him off the trail? "What are you doing here, by the way? How did you get the Wolfmen to respect you enough not to attack you on sight?"

Jaxon's smile seemed to become flirtatious, and he gestured at the collapsible bed he was sitting on. Or was it a padded table of some kind? "Why don't you lay down and I'll show you *exactly* what I can do for you. I've been told that my hands are magical. You'll feel better than you have in *years*."

"Ah. *No*, no thanks." Jess lost any vestige of a smile. How could this filthy man proposition her so blatantly, so publicly? Sicko. What a disgusting waste of space. "When are you going to want to leave here?"

"I would say..." Jaxon looked around at the stronghold, which was swiftly beginning to smell like wet dog. He had no interest in seeing what *drying* dog smelled like here. "As soon as the rain stops?"

CHAPTER TEN

"So, I just wanted to say thank you *once more* for your hospitality!" Jaxon was standing at the back of the stronghold, attempting to get into the wilderness to continue his quest. Unfortunately, several Warriors were blocking his path. "Now that the pleasantries are out of the way, how about you do the same?"

The Warriors chuffed, all three of them standing head and shoulders above the tall Monk. Broken English flowed from a muzzle, "You stay, refine bodies of The People."

Jaxon had learned that the Wolfmen tribes referred to themselves collectively as 'The People'. "Let me put it like this. If *The People* don't get out of *the way*, they are going to meet *the fist.*" He shook a clenched hand at the Warriors to no avail. His intimidation was raging at full power, but the Wolfmen merely chuffed their brand of laughter at him.

"Fine, *fine*, feisty human!" Jaxon's hair was ruffled by a massive paw. "We move. We see you soon anyway. Take look."

The Wolfman gestured expansively, and Jaxon followed his movements to see a huge line of flat terrain curving away into the distance on either side of the stronghold. "You see? Is... *totem guide*. This place is trial, not kill zone. You is get close dead, you show up right there. No fun, though, lose strength, lose memories." Now he pointed at a flat, black rock which was where the line intersected.

"We die or get too close to dying, and we will respawn there instead of our bind point?" Jess gasped at the implication. "We'd *still* lose experience? Jaxon, if I die in there, I die twice."

"Oh, yeah. Is correct." The Warrior nodded at her words and slapped Jaxon gently on the back. Gently for his race anyway. "Female, you come back without this one, we eat well. *Okay!* Cute, little smooth-skins, you go fun have."

Jaxon and Jess watched them go back to their post, and Jaxon shook his head. "Can you believe that? They–"

Jess interrupted in a rush of emotion, "Threatened us? Plan on *eating* me? *Assume* we are going to die out there?"

"–think we're cute!" Jaxon finished blandly. "Hmm? Did you say something?"

Jess shook her head, tongue-tied and confused by this strange man that the Wolfmen seemed to like so much. They clambered over the wall, Jess carefully lowering herself while Jaxon jumped and arrested his movement by flipping in midair and turning the motion into a somersault on the ground. From there, he popped up to his feet and cheered for himself. "He stuck the landing! He's awarded a nine, a nine point five, and *oooh, too bad!* The Russian judge gives him a two!"

"What are you doing?" Jess's words made Jaxon flinch and get into a fighting position.

"*What* in the... oh, right, it's Jess." Jaxon stood straight and brushed some dust off his robe. "Good lord, you *are* a forgettable one, aren't you? As to your question, I spend quite a bit of time alone and have found that monologuing helps to maintain mental alacrity."

Jess simply stared at him with her mouth open, not quite able to believe what an absolute *jerk* this man was. Her fingers twitched toward her empty sheath, angry that she had been disarmed. Wait a second... "Jaxon, I don't have any weapons. We need to go back."

The Monk didn't bother to turn around, simply twirling a hand in the air. "If you want to go back, feel free. I won't be waiting for you, but I'm sure 'The People' will welcome you back with open arms and a wide smile. Otherwise, we are just going to have to make do!"

Jess looked back, indeed seeing a Warrior pointing at her with a wide 'smile'. He made a 'finger across the throat' gesture when they locked eyes. She shuddered and followed Jaxon, who was almost far enough away that the Scouts on the defensive wall would start attacking her. There were whines of disappointment as she got closer to the Monk, and her mood darkened further. Jess needed to make sure she was ready to escape when the moment came. To that end, she lowered her center of balance by crouching and slunk after Jaxon.

To her dismay, he didn't look back a single time as he was walking, and she seriously wondered if he had forgotten that she was walking with him again. When he started speaking aloud, she perked up, excited to have a conversation. Then she heard him start singing, "The foot bone connects to the... *leg bone*! The leg bone connects to the... *knee bone*! The knee bone connects to the... *thigh bone*!"

"Stop singing!" Jess snapped at him. "*Why*? Why are you even singing that song?"

Jaxon looked back, not seeing her even though her noise had partially broken stealth mode. "Who's talking? Oh. Jess. Right. Seriously, can you wear a bell or something? I was singing that children's song because it a pleasing reminder of where my occupation began, even though it is not exactly anatomically accurate. That song has been stuck in my head for... oh, I don't know. Twenty years or so?"

Jess really wanted to know what trick of this game had made her select this crazy man to follow. She promised herself that if she got out of this area, Jaxon was going to be on the receiving side of her daggers even *if* she couldn't loot his body! In fact... he couldn't see her right now. Not at all. She crept forward, her hands going on either side of his head. Not stopping to think, she brutally grabbed him and twisted his head to the side. His eyes were now locked with hers, his head *almost* facing the wrong direction.

Her cold smile at Jaxon's confused look faltered as he started speaking, "Are you licensed for this sort of work? Thanks, but I think I have a higher skill in adjustments than you do. That did absolutely nothing for me."

Face turning pale, Jess stumbled backward and nearly retched as Jaxon's head righted itself, and he kept moving at a brisk pace. He didn't even consider that an *attack*? What kind of *monster* was she traveling with? She went to ask him a question, and her luck wore out. Jaxon's horrendous charisma kicked in, and no matter what it was that she actually said, this is what he heard, "*Jaxon, I crouch all day in stealth mode, and I think it is messing with my posture. Can you help?*"

Jaxon whipped around, face ecstatic and fingers wiggling furiously. "I would *love* to get my hands on you! I'll show you *exactly* how amazing I can make you feel!"

Jess flushed red and dodged away from him as he reached out for her, sure that something either gross or dangerous was occurring. Jaxon was breathing erratically, and all she could think of was that he was suddenly trying to take revenge for her attempt at snapping his neck. "I'm *so* sorry, Jaxon! It won't happen again. I swear I'll be a good travel companion!"

"What? What are you talking about?" Jaxon's fingers stopped shifting slowly, seemingly knowing that they wouldn't be working right now. "Jess, I'm just trying to make you feel good. Isn't that what you wanted?"

"Not... um. Not now, not with you, or in this sort of place." Jess was blushing furiously. Why did *every* man she met fall head over heels for her?

Jaxon looked around at the wilderness they were traversing. There were no paths, the underbrush was knee-high, and they could be attacked at any moment. "I understand. Forgive my lack of forethought. I didn't mean to detract from the experience by doing this right here. Perhaps later, if we can find a nice clearing."

Somehow... somehow Jess was *blushing*! She had never had someone so *serious*, so *invested*, in wooing her this suddenly! The way Jaxon spoke, it was passionate and full of intensity. He *really* wanted her, she could tell. Maybe... perhaps he was just terrible at making small talk? Her thoughts were written on her face, but luckily for her, Jaxon was already walking toward his goal once again. He was grumbling, and she assumed that he was sad that he had been so pushy with her. Too bad for Jess, she was *just* too far away to hear him mumbling about finding proper lumbar support for a makeshift bed this evening.

"Jasmyn, how is your night vision? The sun is beginning to set, and I think we should find a place to rest before we *need* to find one." Jaxon never stopped plodding forward, resigned to moving slowly so his new companion could keep up.

"My night vision is fine, but did you just get my *name* wrong?" Jessamyn stared at the back of Jaxon's head, willing him to turn and face her reignited wrath.

The Monk didn't respond, simply nodding along at whatever he heard her 'say'. "I see, I see. It must have been terrible for you to be out in the woods so long by yourself!"

"Hey! I'm telling you that I am fine to keep moving at night!" Jess tried to get his attention by being too loud.

"Oh? Thank you for pointing that out." Jaxon looked back at her. "I wouldn't have even seen that clearing, good catch!"

"You upset me with your illogic." Jess resigned herself to one-sided conversations for the foreseeable future.

Jaxon walked into the clearing—brushing against a tree—and was grabbed by Jess and yanked backward as a massive branch slammed into the ground where he had been about to walk. He caught his balance easily; having a raw score of one hundred dexterity wasn't just for show. Jaxon watched as the branch lifted into the air, vanishing into the foliage above them. "Did you see which tree that was, by chance? I was slightly too distracted to note it."

"I have a concerning thought." Jess grimly bent over and grabbed a rock, tossing it against a tree a bit further away. As the small stone bounced off the wood, a branch smashed into the spot it had touched. "It looks like we aren't allowed to climb trees to seek shelter. It looks like we are going to be forced to stay on the ground and fight whatever is alive in this forest."

Just then, a songbird alighted on a tree and was whipped with a twig. All that remained was a poof of slowly falling feathers. Jaxon nodded seriously. "I had been wondering why I hadn't heard any birds in the last hour."

CHAPTER ELEVEN

Jess and Jaxon had decided to keep moving, hoping to find a more defensible location than an open clearing. As the light faded further, their pace began to slow. Jaxon looked over at Jess as she straightened up, the back crackling had caused him to almost begin drooling.

Jess saw him looking at her with a flushed face and got the wrong idea once again. "You seriously aren't going to be able to focus unless we do this, are you?"

"I... I don't think I will," Jaxon admitted, swallowing and inspecting her closely. She blushed a flaming red, looking down and muttering.

"I think you're pretty cute too, and I guess this *is* just a game..." She looked up at Jaxon with a sultry expression on her face. "Alright, let's do this. You need to get your head straight, and it's been a long time for me, too."

"Are you sure? Right here in the forest?" Jaxon's smile had stretched across his face, distorting his expression to an almost inhuman level.

"You have that bed thing?" Jess's words were barely out of her mouth when Jaxon was unfurling his chiropractic table and getting ready. She sat down and looked up at him as he came close. "I can't believe I'm doing this. I *never* do this sort of thing."

"That's okay; I just hope that I get you interested in doing this more often, especially in real life." Jaxon motioned for her to lay down. "Lay on your front?"

Jess was beet red as she lay down languidly. "I just can't believe– *Gah!*"

You have been paralyzed! Time remaining: 10... 9...

"Adjust!" *Crack*! Jaxon efficiently adjusted the lady; properly aligning her head, spine, and limbs for the first time in her character's life. "Adjust! Adjust! *Adjust*."

Crack! *Crack*! *Crack*!

Jess's health dropped by a tenth on the final adjustment. As Jaxon stepped back, the paralysis wore off, and she flipped off the table and flew at Jaxon with her hands stretched into claws. "I'm going to *murder* you!"

Jaxon easily dodged out of the way and avoided the subsequent attacks. "What in the *world* are you doing? Why do people keep attacking me after I help them? Oh! I *see*! You are testing out your new levels of dexterity and strength on someone you can't really hope to hurt! That's fine then, but I don't know if this is the best location or time to do that. The sun is going down."

Jess didn't respond, firmly set on tearing chunks of bleeding meat out of this infuriating and confusing man! The most frustrating part? He was *right*. She couldn't land a single hit on him. "Stop *moving* so I can *kill* you!"

"Why would I do *that*?" Jaxon was hardly needing to use any effort to avoid her attacks but was starting to realize that she was attacking him in earnest.

"I thought we were going to...! We were...!" Jess couldn't properly form a sentence; she was *frothing* mad and blushing the darkest red Jaxon had ever seen.

"What? Oh! *Ohh*..." Jaxon shook his head and did a double backward handspring, keeping his feet flat on the ground until his palms were touching the ground and vice versa until he was in a normal position again. "Oh, *sweetheart*, I didn't realize. I *really* didn't. I haven't been propositioned in... what, going on thirty-five years now?"

"*I* propositioned *you*?" Jess stopped attacking, his words penetrating her thoughts and blowing away all her expectations of humiliation or ridicule. "Who *are* you?"

"My name is Jaxon. I am a Chiropractor." Jaxon bowed in half without moving his feet or bending his lower half at all, making Jess feel ill. Human bodies weren't supposed to move like that. "I am ninety-two years old and have been stuck in a room doing research ever since I sold my practice twenty years ago. When this game came out, it gave me a chance at *finally* forwarding my research legally, as well as allowing me to reclaim the body I had in my youth. I wasted it then, and I decided that I wouldn't make the same mistake again. I feel *terrible* for this misunderstanding. Truly, I do."

At that point, as Jess was gathering her wits to form a decent reply, Jaxon saw a system message he had never seen before.

Due to a special action and extreme effort, you have trained a characteristic point! Charisma +1!

"Why did that message have all that extra floof?" Jaxon was more startled by that fact than the actual gain. "Normally, it just says the stat and 'plus whatever'. Ah, I see you are confused. I just gained twenty-five percent more charisma than I had before this moment."

"You got a boost of *a quarter*?" Jess calmed down, trying to understand the issues at hand with logic instead of stabbing. "Wait. Jaxon, what is your raw score for charisma?"

"Five," he responded instantly, obviously pleased by this upgrade. "I hadn't gained more than a single point in the entirety of traveling with my usual companions, but I gained that in the first day of knowing you! There must be something *special* about you."

Jess slunk back, his words touching on her nerves after this whole incident. "I see. No wonder people have such trouble around you. Now I'm not surprised that the Wolfmen liked you! I guess they have the same type of manners, so it makes sense."

Jaxon opened his mouth to respond, snapping his jaw shut as a message appeared in his vision.

Night has arrived in the forest of trials. Doubling the number of predatory monsters in the zone. Good luck on your survival!

"I do not like the sound of that." Jaxon continued looking around for a location they could defend. Nothing appeared, just like all the other times. It was almost as if this area were intentionally cleared of any beneficial structures, caves, or other such easy survival options. "Why don't we hunker down in the underbrush and see if we can't get some sleep? Even if the number of monsters in the area is doubled, we still haven't actually seen any."

"Are you kidding right now, old man? We're being stalked by at *least* four monsters! They are right on the edge of my visual range, and every time I stop paying attention to them, they dart toward us."

"*What?* Where?" Jaxon flailed around in the deepening darkness, his uncontrolled hands cracking like whips as he made sharp turns and sudden changes to his speed. Not seeing anything, even though the creatures were watching him hungrily, Jaxon snorted and blew a raspberry. "Whippersnappers, making up stories to scare people! You're the girl who cried Wolfman!"

Right then, Jess realized that she could escape him right now if she wanted to. There would be no witnesses, and the darkness impeding his already low perception would ensure that the Monk was claimed by the wildlife. This thought was instantly countered by another. She had *also* realized that this was the first time since she had started playing that she was having fun. Jaxon was strange, infuriating, and *incredibly* vexing... but he was also genuine, straightforward, and frankly hilarious now that she understood where he was coming from with his outdated humor. Old men were adorable.

"If I'm going to stay with him, I need to do it properly." She winced as she opened the social tab in her status window and left the party that she was in. Without the option to track her, they should never be able to find them in the wilderness. "There goes getting into *that* guild. Maybe it's for the best. I'd feel too bad about robbing someone's Grandpa."

"What are you mumbling about to yourself over there? Whatever, I'm going to take a nap. Stand watch, will you?" Jaxon started settling down onto the ground, and Jess's eyes went wide as the darkness-cloaked beasts darted in.

"Jaxon, *look out!*" Jaxon hopped up from the ground, spinning in place like a blender and smacking away clawed hands to the sound of loud screeching. As the creatures got close to the Monk, they were easily identified as some form of monkey, possibly a variant of a howler monkey from the sound they began releasing as soon as their sneak attack failed.

Ah-whooo! The throaty howls shattered the still night air; the sound repeated in the distance and echoed through the forest. The cries were full of rage and excitement as the monkeys called their brethren, their message clear: a challenger had arrived... and it was dinner time.

CHAPTER TWELVE

Unable to protect himself by having a tree situated behind him, Jaxon was taken to the ground as a monkey jumped silently at his back. Since he had been focused on the ones attacking from his front and Jess hadn't been able to call out a warning, Jaxon was now on the ground being savagely torn into by various-sized animals. Jess was having her own troubles, being unarmed and under attack by the most agile of the monkeys. They were the only ones who could keep up with her movements, and none of them would have been able to land a blow on Jaxon if he were able to see where they were coming from before they landed on him.

Jaxon was losing health rapidly since his constitution was fairly low for a front-line fighter of his level, but he had finally been able to secure solid positioning for himself. He pushed himself to the side, knocking over several monkeys and escaping the claws of the others. Jaxon had torn skin that was flopping about as he moved, each motion releasing a spurt of blood. As he whirled around to dodge another leaping monkey, he struck out and buried his stiffened fingers into its yielding flesh.

"Yes! The bone is right there, as it should be!" Jaxon slammed his palms into the animal as it landed on the ground, as much to damage it as to feel out its joint structure. "The bones are elongated but otherwise similar enough to a human. I can begin the *procedure*."

The needles in his gloves penetrated the joint deeply on his third attack, slicing open cartilage and severely reducing the monkey's usage of that limb. Then he needed to move again as the others came to the rescue of the screaming simian. Jaxon bent his head backward as claws lashed out in an attempt to tear out his eyes. Using the momentum of dodging to his advantage, he grabbed and tossed the offender over him and into a tree. There was a crashing of wood, and the animal was reduced to a paste as a massive wooden limb smashed down repeatedly.

"I like that *quite* a lot!" Jaxon laughed as he shifted away from his typical strategy. Instead of working on each patient individually and giving them the proper care and assistance they needed, he worked to disable one and fend off the others until he could throw one at a tree. When the fourth monkey was destroyed by the environment, the other six retreated, screaming and howling. Once again, the sound was repeated by their fellow predators, much closer this time. "Jess, we need to leave! Jess?"

Jaxon looked around with deep disappointment. Ah well, if she hadn't been able to survive until this point, perhaps it was for the best that she... Jess stepped out of the underbrush, breathing heavily. She had several shallow cuts on her, though nothing like Jaxon's somewhat grievous wounds.

Experience gained: 100 (25 * Trial Primate x4)

Health: 312/400 Status ailment: Bleeding (Heavy) -10 hp per minute until wound has been closed.

"You doing alright there, Jess?" Jaxon held a couple of the deepest gashes together, using one of his acupuncture needles to artificially staple the flaps of skin together. After he had done this to the worst offenders, he saw that his ailment had been reduced to 'bleeding moderately heavy' and he was now only losing seven health per minute. He pressed on his arms, and the bleeding slowed further as his acupressure shifted his blood flow.

"I'm fine, Jaxon." Jess brushed a few leaves off her shirt and took a deep breath. "If we can't sleep here, let's log off and meet up again in the morning, alright? I don't think it'd be smart to continue on in the dark."

"Fair enough." Jaxon opened his screen, tapping the logout button.

Warning! Logging off while in this area will return you to the most recent position outside of the trial area. This will count as a death. Are you sure you'd like to continue? Yes / No.

"It seems that is not a valid plan." Jaxon looked over at Jess as the howling began to increase in pitch and volume. "I think that we should instead attempt to run for it. Can you lead the way without getting us in trouble?"

"No promises on the trouble, but I have a map and compass permanently set in my vision, so I can at least guide us." Jess turned and started walking. Jaxon was glad to hear her words; he had planned to go a different direction entirely! It seemed that she was indeed a positive investment toward his future success. "There are monkeys following us, but they are staying back for now. I think they will only attack when enough of them arrive to cause us serious issues. When enough are killed, they back off. Now, I can't ensure that is the truth, but it is what I have seen in combat to this point."

"Ah, do you have plans to be a battlemaster or tactician?" Jaxon asked approvingly. "That was an excellent assessment of our current predicament and highlighted points I had not thought of. If you would like a recommendation to my guild when we leave here, I would be happy to do that for you."

Jess looked back at him briefly, giving him the faintest of smiles. "Thanks, Jaxon, that might be nice. I doubt I would want into your guild, but what one is it?"

"The Wanderer's Guild." Jaxon's words made Jess miss her footing and trip over an exposed root. Luckily, the tree did not seem to take offense to this, and no branches came whipping at them. "I too did not think there would be great benefit from joining but was pleasantly surprised at the swift increases in level and access to decent gear. I'd recommend thinking on it if you are interested at all."

"You are in one of the *Noble Guilds*?" Jess went quiet for a moment, focusing on pushing through the underbrush and staying ahead of the other roving bands of monkeys that she was certain were out there. So far, the ones trailing them hadn't made any threatening moves, but they would let out a deep bellow every once in a while to alert the others to their location. "I can honestly say that I'm glad I met you now. I'd love to get into that guild... if it is at all possible."

"All I can do is make the request." Jaxon shrugged expansively, an interesting sight on a man who was hopping over blackberry bushes. "We need to finish this first, though. My bleeding debuff has vanished, but I have lost a significant amount of health. What do you suggest we do from here?"

"We should keep moving until daylight and hope that we can lose our pursuers," Jess stated frankly.

"Are you sure?" Jaxon looked at her, barely able to make out her outline in the darkness. "Alright, I guess! Stand and fight it is!"

"Wait, no, what?" She had already taken another dozen strides, but Jaxon's sudden stop and whirl had also caught their followers off guard. He was already amongst their troop and had dislocated all four limbs of one of them and started in on the second. The first was wailing on the ground unable to do more than flop around in agony as his tormentor beat down the others.

Only four creatures had been following them; the others were too damaged or already dead. Jaxon reduced that number down to one with an extra *twist*, and it ran off into the forest howling. He would have given chase but decided that it was more important to finish off the others first.

Experience gained: 75 (25 * Trial Primate x3)

Looking at the elongated claws of the primates cooling on the ground, Jaxon had a sudden idea. He poked the wrist over and over, finally activating adjust and watching the monkey paw pop off the hairy arm. He picked it up, inspected it, then took another paw before handing them both to Jess.

Item gained: Trial Primate Paw (Trash). While not useful in a traditional sense, this paw can be used in lieu of small blades or slashing weapons. Adds +10 slashing damage on hit with a 20% chance to cause bleeding on a critical hit.

"What are these for?" Jess inspected the blood-dripping paws with disgust.

"Those are your new weapons!" Jaxon patted her on the arm, leaving behind a bloody handprint. She flinched away as the wet warmth registered. "You don't have anything better, so we gotta make due. We should also get going before others find us."

Jess gingerly held the makeshift weapons, trying to find a good way to use them without getting covered in gore. "I hate this so much."

"Come *on*, Jess. We need to get moving." Jaxon smiled at her disconcertingly. "Stop monkeying around."

"I'll cut you."

CHAPTER THIRTEEN

"I don't know how mush longer I can go on, 'axon." Jess's words were slurring, and she was swaying on her feet. "I'm... I'm so tired. And thirsty. An' I could really go for a nap."

"We've only been awake for two days straight and moving the entire time with very little food or drink. We've got this." Jaxon tried to smile winningly, but at that moment, he received another debuff and his smile came out as a horrific sneer toward his partner.

Debuff: Sleep Deprivation (Rank three). Your constitution is not high enough to sustain the lack of sleep you have been accruing. Current impact: -15% all raw characteristics, rounded down to the nearest whole. -20% Skill experience gained. +20% Experience gained.

"Did you know that we gain extra experience right now? That's exciting, isn't it?" Jaxon prodded Jess to get her moving again, the short stop causing her head to droop—almost sending her into an unconscious state. "Since I'm already a Master of the things I really care about, I'm fine with the skill point loss. Too bad about the loss of stats, though. That puts my dexterity all the way down to eighty-five. I won't be able to escape the primates when it gets dark again." Jaxon was half-carrying the Scout as she stumbled forward. She was hardly moving of her own volition, the loss to her stats dropping her endurance—and therefore stamina—to untenable levels.

Jaxon was barely able to keep going on his own, and Jess was slipping further and further toward the ground. The monkeys were on their tail again; they must have come across a blood trail. Hooting and screeching were resounding through the woods, and Jaxon wasn't sure if they were going to make it. He blinked away tears, not from sadness but from the sudden and intense sunshine that flooded over him. Looking around, he blinked away the pain and tried to understand what he was seeing.

A white structure stood on top of a hill *almost* large enough to be called a mountain. The building itself appeared to be a temple of some sort, and Jaxon realized that they had found their destination! All they needed to do now was survive long enough to reach it. "Jess! Jess, we are here! You need to wake up. There's a steep incline here. I can't carry you up!"

Jess mumbled something incoherently, continuing to slide down. When she was almost to her knees, Jaxon heard her speak clearly, "*You should go on without me or find a way to force me to wake up. Otherwise, I'm going to stay here.*"

"I hope you are sure about this." Jaxon pulled out an extra-long acupuncture needle. "The process of waking someone up is not approved, and if I were to do this in a coma ward, I would be put in jail. It is going to *hurt.*"

Jess was somehow breathing deeply and regularly even as she responded, "*Go for it, Jaxon! It's the only way.*"

"I agree. Let's begin." Jaxon stood behind her, holding her head steady with his left hand as the long needle in his right came closer to her neck. "I am about to insert this needle into your brachial plexus, so make sure not to move until it is out. I have no plans to cause you permanent injury, and I'm not sure what all the world here will fix without outside intervention."

The needle jabbed deeply into Jess's muscle, stimulating her nerves and sending intense and shooting pain through her. Jaxon had already removed the needle by the time she was able to consciously react, so as she shot upright and whirled to face him, all she saw was the man staring at her with an excited expression and a too-wide, snarling smile. His next words confused her further, especially since his lips were twisting in ways that didn't seem to make the words that he was saying. "*Did that hurt? Good! Maybe now you will be able to move yourself, and I won't need to do all the work!*"

"Jaxon!" Jess teared up, the stress of no sleep and his cold words sending her mood spinning. "Why are you being so cruel?"

Jaxon looked at her with a vicious sneer. "Cruel? I'm not being *cruel.* You are just sleep deprived and not listening to me correctly! I'm trying to be realistic. I can't get you up *that!*"

For the first time, Jess looked at their location and realized that something else was going on. They were at the temple! Well, almost. She nodded at him tiredly, the pain in her neck and shoulder beginning to fade rapidly as the muscles stopped spasming. "I understand that you had to make me wake up, but promise me you won't do something like that again!"

"No can do." Jaxon shook his head as he began carefully climbing the steep hill. He had to be on all fours in order to not fall, but he seemed to be in his element. Jaxon rapidly began moving up toward the temple, calling down behind him, "What if another situation arises like this? Where a little pain saves you from being torn apart? Can't promise that I won't save you! Also, there are animals coming. You should probably get moving!"

The howls were getting much closer, and from his vantage point, Jaxon was able to see flashes of fur through the trees. Thank goodness it was still daytime! Jess tried climbing the hill without going onto all fours, but she quickly found that keeping her balance was near impossible, even with her high dexterity. Since Jaxon wasn't looking at her, she gave in and started bear-crawling up the incline. She slipped several times, the current reduction to her stats making her far less capable than she felt she truly was.

Jess looked down, a mistake as she realized two things: one, she was already much higher than she had thought she was. Two, the primates had left the woods and were congregating at the base of the hill. They stopped there, watching and waiting. Each time she slipped, they began to howl and hop up and down. By slipping, scree would be disturbed, and loose stone would tumble down to where the animals waited. The rocks started coming back *up* as the monkeys began chucking them as accurately as they could. One clipped her as it bounced off another rock, opening a gash on her forehead that began bleeding profusely into her eyes. She wiped away the blood, almost slipping again as her moist hand lost traction.

"We are almost to the top, Jess!" Jaxon called back to her. She looked up, expecting to see the temple looming over her, instead finding that they hadn't even moved a quarter of the way up the rocky face of the hill. "You know, in comparison to the last few days of travel. We are infinitely closer!"

"Why did I try traps? Why didn't I just sneak up on him and stab his kidneys until they were exposed to the open air? He couldn't have even done anything about it!" Jess muttered under her breath, gasping from exertion. She started needing to pause and let her stamina refill, and each time she did so, there was a chance she would simply fall asleep.

"Jess! *Jess!*" Jaxon's words shattered her thoughts, and she realized that she was laying down on the hill. She had started slipping downward as well and needed to scrabble to arrest her momentum. That was only a part of why Jaxon had started yelling, though. "Behind you!"

Jess looked back and saw that there were nearly a hundred primates gathered at the base of the hill, and they had just started *climbing*. Luckily, the ascent was very steep and rocky. Where there wasn't a handhold, the rock was quite smooth. The primates were moving faster than she was but not by much. If she were to get moving, they *shouldn't* be able to catch her. Jess got going, looking up to see Jaxon over halfway to the top. "How did you get so far up there?"

His reply came floating down to her, making Jess grind her teeth, "Continuous effort!"

Her stamina recovered slightly, Jess started climbing upward. Jaxon watched her for a moment, then nodded. She was focused now. Even though the pain was no longer keeping her awake, her willpower and survival instinct should be working together to keep her moving. He looked up, not at the temple but at the position of the sun. "Maybe an hour before sunset? I could make it, I could make it easily, but..."

Jaxon looked down where the simians were climbing and starting to throw rocks again. Actually, from the way the projectiles splattered and stuck, not everything being thrown was a rock. With one last glance at the edge of the hill, he made his decision and waited. He wasn't going to go *down*—just in case she fell or was overtaken—but when she got *here,* he would do what he could to help her the rest of the way. The wait was torturous for him, and nearly half the time remaining for daylight had slipped away by the time she was level with him.

"Why didn't you keep going?" Her words came between gasping breaths. Jess's arms were shaking, and their pursuers were closing in behind them.

"Gotta make sure we both make it there. We may not be a party, but that doesn't mean I am fine with watching you get torn apart and eaten by monkeys with feces-coated claws." Jaxon smiled winningly at her, but her head drooped and she lightly tapped her forehead on the rock below.

"Sometimes I just don't know about you, Jaxon," Jess whispered with deep exasperation. He reached over to her; she was looking forward to some human contact, but all he did was pluck a stone out of the air that had been aimed at her head.

"Nasty creatures." Jaxon slid down a few feet, taking the lead beasts by surprise with a couple solid kicks. They started tumbling down the slope, taking a few others with them as they careened down to the base of the hill. "Make sure not to slip or let them grab you. I'm not too excited about attempting to climb this again."

The monkeys, understanding the danger posed by falling, were now spreading out and attempting to get ahead of the humans. Jaxon and Jess began scrambling up the slope, intent on staying ahead and alive. Twice, one of the primates got ahead of them, but working together, the small group was able to fend off the attacks and keep themselves from falling. Sunset came and went, the darkness settling in on them making the climb even more treacherous.

They were almost to the top, but the climb had become almost vertical. They needed to rest before attempting to continue, and so spent a few minutes sending the monkeys tumbling down the slopes. When they had a good five feet of space, they began scaling the rock. Jaxon was *certain* they were going to fall, but then his hand slapped down on *horizontal* stone! He pulled himself over the ledge, taking a deep breath before reaching back and grabbing Jess's hand. With a grunt of exertion, he pulled her to relative safety.

CHAPTER FOURTEEN

"We made it." Jess flopped directly to the ground as she came over the ledge. She wanted to move, but she was far too exhausted to make the effort. "The... the monkeys?"

Jaxon crawled to the edge and looked over. "They are still there, but they seem disappointed. It seems they aren't coming any closer, but they *are* gathering together on the slope and staring up at us. I'm surprised that they weren't able to overwhelm us with their speed on the incline... perhaps their long claws made climbing the stone a difficult activity."

He paused, then shouted over the edge, "I'm sorry you are going hungry down there!"

Jess stared up at the stars and shook her head. "Do you even think through what you are saying? They would be eating *us* if they weren't going hungry. Just... are we safe right now? Did they stop following us because we are getting close to something more dangerous, or can I sleep?"

"This close to the edge?" Jaxon shook his head. "Two issues there. You might fall off the ledge, or something might attack us. We should... you're asleep. Drat. Alright, well, let's hope for the best then."

Jaxon flopped onto the ground next to Jess and closed his eyes, his 'exhausted' debuff ensuring that he was asleep in moments. The bare stone wasn't going to be the best bed, but neither of them was in a position to complain. The primates below them seemed to sense that the humans had fallen asleep and began screeching in frustration. The noise didn't bother the unconscious people in the slightest, but both of them shifted uneasily in their sleep as a powerful, foreign gaze swept over their prone figures.

Hours passed in moments, at least to Jaxon's perceptions. His fingers began twitching, unsurprisingly the first sign of wakefulness in the Monk. After a few moments, his eyes popped open and he heaved himself upright. Since he didn't use his hands, instead simply pulling his muscles tight and arriving on his feet, Jess cursed and stumbled away from him. "Jaxon! That was some horror movie crap right there!"

Jaxon looked over at her, blinked owlishly and looked around the plateau they were standing on. "Full daylight? Dehydration is starting to kick in heavily. Laying in the noontime sun didn't help this at all. Hunger is becoming extreme. I wouldn't be surprised if I started losing stats due to this. Sleep deprivation is cleared, but I have no 'rested' bonus. No attacks over the time sleeping, so we must be in a safe zone or the predator of this area wasn't around."

He suddenly began contorting, his bones cracking and his body shifting. A few moments later, Jaxon glanced at Jess once more and smiled brightly. "Good morning, Jess. I was just looking myself over and taking stock of the situation. Didn't mean to ignore you! By chance did you see that we are next to the temple?"

"It... yeah it was hard to miss that." Jess gestured at the wall of white stone they had slept next to. "Any plans on what we should do next?"

Jaxon looked up at the sheer, white wall, scratched his chin, and let his head drift back and forth. "I suppose we should look for an entrance. Would you like to travel around together or go our separate ways?"

"Would you even find the door if I left you alone to look for it?"

"I'm certain I would be fine." Jaxon nodded gravely. "I do have a raw score of twenty-one points in perception. My only real issue comes from things that are hiding or hidden. It isn't like I can't see things as obvious as a door or small gate."

"Whatever." Jess grumpily stomped around the exterior of the building with Jaxon skipping along behind her. They went a quarter of the way around the medium-sized temple before they found something different on the pure white stone. "Is that an outline?"

"I think so!" Jaxon started closing in on the wall. "If my prior experience with games is any indication, that means we need to smash the wall right here!"

"Wait, no...!" Jess called futilely as Jaxon swung a fist at the stone. Just before he touched it, the wall opened up into a hallway.

"Oh, look! I found the door." Jaxon took a step into the temple, and the wall closed behind him. Jess let out a strangled cry and ran forward. In less than a second, she was at the wall, and it opened up to admit her. Unsurprisingly, Jaxon was nowhere to be found. Jess sighed and stepped through the wall.

"I suppose this would be a good way to see what I'm capable of on my own." She marched inward as the wall sealed behind her.

As Jess walked forward into the temple, Jaxon was just finishing his fall down a steep ramp that had opened beneath him upon his entry to the building. It leveled out into a slick slide near the bottom, and Jaxon skid halfway across the room he was in before finally coming to a stop. He hopped to his feet and brushed himself off before looking around. Jaxon's gaze stopped on the only source of light in the room, a shining, golden eye. After a full second of staring at each other, the eye winked out, and the room began to brighten until it was nearing predawn lumination. A screen appeared in front of Jaxon's face, refusing to vanish until Jaxon had read through the entire thing.

Welcome Challenger! You have entered the Temple of Tempering! By reaching this location, you have passed the first test. From this point forward, the longer you survive, the greater your rewards will be. When you die, you will be placed in front of the temple and barred from reentering the solo halls. Do your best, for you will not have another chance. The countdown to your death begins... now!

The screen vanished, and Jaxon blinked at the gloomy area around him, his night vision impacted but his heart soaring. He was surrounded on all sides by animate skeletons, and he had never been happier. "Bones! Human bones! Look at the way they articulate! They are moving as though bound by flesh, but the movements are visible!"

Sharp fingertips reached for his face, but he easily brushed them away with an aggressive wave of his own hand. "I have so many theories to test! First, I need to ensure these will be affected in the same manner as a living person, and I also need to make sure I'm not overrun. I am sorry to those of you this will impact, but I need to destroy at least half of this group. I assure you that your sacrifice will not be in vain!"

The skeletons didn't respond beyond a slight pause at his words. Their rictus grins were the first Jaxon had seen that shone with the same clarity and excitement as his own, so he was not going to waste the opportunity to improve his craft. They were already on him, so it was a simple matter to begin inserting his fingers into bone sockets and using his knuckles to apply sudden pressure and torsion to joints. With every blow he dealt, Jaxon studied his opponents. In return, they began to take a toll of flesh and blood. They weren't overly strong, but the magic animating them seemed to make them inordinately sturdy. If they had been able to put weight behind their attacks, the thousand gashes and cuts he was receiving would have instead reduced him to a pulp.

"This is ineffectual." Jaxon activated Adjust one last time, and his targeted skeleton's head spun in place on its spine before simply coming to rest in its original location. Then it attempted to punch him in the face with spiked knuckles. Jaxon dodged the blow easily even as another dozen weak fists pounded across his body. "It seems dismantling is my only option at this point. Off with his head!"

A swift uppercut sent the empty skull flying away. The remainder of the skeleton collapsed to the ground, as whatever magic had been holding it together failed. Smashing the skull or removing it was the only way to reliably stop the skeletons from coming after him, and he preferred to remove the skulls just in case he could reanimate a full skeleton for later experimentation. Having determined the best course of action, Jaxon pushed back and rolled over the top of the massed undead. Now with the majority of his targets in front of him, the Monk was easily able to begin separating their heads from bodies.

A pile of intact skulls grew on the outskirts of combat, while the collapsing bodies began to make footing tricky. Jaxon turned and punched, dodged multiple fists, and had soon cleared half of the enemies. He hopped backward a few feet and looked at the current situation. He had a respectable pile of undamaged skulls but hadn't been able to stop himself from destroying nearly a third of them. He paused too long, and his notifications decided it was time to pop out at him.

*Exp: 36 (1 * Skeleton x36).*

"You are all level one?" Jaxon paused and paid attention as an undamaged skeleton strode toward him and took a swing. It hit him in the face, opening a shallow cut on his cheek.

-1 HP

"You *are* level one. Well... that makes this easier." Jaxon stepped into the group and began *punching*. No fancy tricks, no attempts at skill usage, just a simple full-strength blow to the skull. The bone crumbled, and he sighed. "Of *course* it is that easy."

Three more were smashed in as many seconds, since the hard part of destroying them was *getting* to them quickly. Now knowing what he was facing, Jaxon looked around the remaining half of the skeletons and matched their grins with his own. "As for the rest of you... let's play."

CHAPTER FIFTEEN

Kneeling down, Jaxon sifted through the bones of a hundred defeated skeletons and tried to separate them into full figures. Pulling over an intact skull, he connected it to a spine and stepped back. The skeleton smoothly stood and began coming after him.

"Good, that worked exactly as I had hoped it would." He studied the murderous framework of a body and tried to memorize every movement it made. It was one thing to watch a body move and assume how the bones moved, but this allowed him to see it at a much more accurate level than even computer modeling had allowed for. He was close to a breakthrough; he just *knew* it.

Jaxon ignored the attacks coming his way; his health regeneration would be more than up to the task of healing him when he was through here. He poked at the skeleton, prodded, twisted, turned, and adjusted it. In his excitement, it wasn't too long before the entire thing suddenly broke into several pieces per bone. This was startling, and no matter how Jaxon thought about it, he had no choice but to concede that this wasn't normal. "Is it... could it be that these things have a structural integrity, and when they take enough damage they simply fall apart?"

There was no other easy explanation for this phenomenon, but of course it needed to be tested. Six skeletons later, he was fairly certain of his hypothesis. Next, he tried to focus on his other theories. The question was: how to gain insight into something that he was already an Expert of? Insight? In. Sight. Jaxon stepped into the next attack coming at him, keeping the fist at eye level as it came close. There was a **crunch** as the skeleton struck him, and he was sure that he had taken a critical hit... but he saw something that he never had before. Jaxon saw the way the bones curled, moved, and the effect absorbing and releasing kinetic energy had when landing a blow.

Skill increased: Human anatomy (Expert IV).

And there it was, a way to study anatomy that he had never attempted before. Who in their right mind would allow someone to punch them in the face and forcibly hold their eyes open to see the movements? Right then, Jaxon understood that he was going to be in for a lot of pain in the near future. Was this a reliable way to close in on the Master ranks? If so, it would be worth every agonizing moment, and no one would be able to convince him otherwise.

Still, he had just been punched in the face. Jaxon backhanded the skeleton so hard that he shattered the entire front of its face. He winced before shrugging and leaning over to combine a skull with a skeleton once again. He paused, and Jaxon glanced at his health bar; noting that he was down to two hundred and twelve of his available four hundred points. He had not taken the time yet to sit down and recover, and so he did so now. Breathing deeply, he attempted to achieve a meditation skill. So far, he had achieved no success with this particular skill set. Perhaps today would be the day? A half hour passed as he relaxed on the floor surrounded by bones. As his health bar topped off, he opened his eyes in disappointment. No luck with the meditation skill today!

Instead of ruminating on his failure, Jaxon did the practical thing and got back to work. Within moments, another skeleton was swinging its bony fist at his face. Jaxon allowed the impact, slightly changing the angle and bone that hit his face first. In this manner, he was able to see nearly every position of a closed right fist as it drilled into his soft flesh. The issue with this method of training was the intense pain and slow-building rage. Jaxon was able to control himself enough to pop the skull off of the spine but then took his impotent fury out on the bones that clattered to the ground. No matter, there were skeletons aplenty and not nearly enough skulls to survive the catharsis that he needed.

A single level one skeleton hitting him in the face over and over had reduced his health by half. Every single blow must have been a critical hit, and Jaxon was feeling it. He resumed his position on the floor, once more closing his eyes and attempting to achieve a proper meditation. Yet again, as his health reached full, there was no notification of success. This cycle repeated several times as he worked to study a left fist hitting him in the face. By the time he was satisfied that he had learned all he could from a closed hand, he was almost ready to move on. Only by forcibly calming himself did he realize that this may be the only opportunity he really had to study moving skeletons in detail. He would not squander this.

For his next test, Jaxon used a leather thong to tie the finger bones back and into a rigid position. While this was not an ideal solution, he could not think of another way to stop the skeletons from punching instead of slapping. Once again, he suffered several hours of pain and regeneration. For his study, for science, he would do far more than this. When he held a firm grasp on the potential bending movements of fingers, he removed the hands from the next skeleton before animating it. From there, he allowed himself to be struck in the face with elbows, forearms, and shoulder strikes.

He must have spent over a day allowing himself to be attacked, and twice, the flaming eye had appeared in the room with him and stared for a few minutes before vanishing. Even a random construct was judging him; he just knew it. By the time he had finished allowing himself to be kicked, kneed, tackled, pushed, and head-butted, he really and truly believed that he had learned everything he could from this method of study. He checked the skill, pleased with the advance.

Skill increased: Human anatomy (Expert VII).

This was progressing slower than he had wanted it to, but it was understandable as human anatomy is more than just skeletal structure. If anything, it was a much more advanced skill. Jaxon assumed that if he wanted to achieve the Master ranks naturally, he would need to study everything from bones to nerves to the meaty portions of a body. That was without understanding the deeper things, such as how food would affect metabolism and bodily processes. Unless he wanted to spend years learning every fact he could, he would need to finish off the progression of the skill with skill points. He was not yet ready to do that for this non-main focus, but depending on his specialization it may be beneficial to do so in the future.

Jaxon stood and crushed every skull that was waiting in the pile. Only then did he get actual notifications of experience gain, in total and counting the skeletons he had defeated before: one hundred points. This meant there had been a full century of enemies to fight. Would the next room also contain a hundred enemies? Would they be level two? If so, even if he were able to defeat that room, he would have a lot of trouble very shortly. As he approached the door, a screen appeared in his vision.

Congratulations, Challenger! You have set the record for the slowest ever recorded traversal of the first solo survival room. There is no benefit for this. We simply thought it was prudent to let you know. Before opening this door, be sure you are rested and prepared for what lies ahead. Rarity of final reward increased by 1% for completing the room.

"Well, what *does* lie ahead?" Even though he was sure he asked the question out loud, Jaxon received no answer. He *was* quite tired and was thankful for the reminder, so he decided to take a short nap before entering the next room. With his stamina and health maximized and any fatigue debuff that may have been creeping up on him taken care of, he stepped forward and opened the door. Jaxon saw what was waiting for him and screamed bloody murder.

"I *hate* bugs!" Jaxon screeched even as he charged forward. Scarab beetles were pouring from holes all throughout the room, moving toward him in an orderly fashion which made the entire room appear to rock and wave. "Great. Disgusting, filthy bugs with a side of seasickness. I had wondered why these trials were supposed to be so difficult. Finally, I understand!"

His *fully* justified rant complete, Jaxon ran into the room and started stomping. Never before had he been so grateful for the entomologist title and its bonus damage to bugs. Before long, he was covered in ichor, chitin, and juices that he had no name or understanding for. His boots were shredded from the sharp exoskeletons and pincers; checking their durability revealed that they were down to two points remaining. He really hoped the next enemy he faced would be something more suiting his skills. Perhaps there would be another room full of skeletons? He perked up at that thought and started toward the door.

Exp: 100 (2 * Scarab beetle x50).

Congratulations, Challenger! In a surprising turn of events, you have set the record for fastest time through the second solo survival room. Rarity of final reward increased by 5% for completing the room with a record.

CHAPTER SIXTEEN

"This is where the trail went dark. I don't know what is going through her mind, but Jess is going to pay for trying to run off on us." The leather-clad Rogue stood back up, reaching his full height at just over six feet tall. His mouth was tightened with displeasure, and his narrow eyes revealed the depths of his anger. "Bring me the animal."

A female Wolfman covered in blood and wounds was dragged to the front of the group. The Rogue looked at her with a sneer, then reached forward and forced her to look into his eyes. "What are we getting into? What is this place, and where would they go from here? Jess is a gold digger. There has to be something in this area she would want."

The proud Wolfman had been reduced to a mere traveling guide after being captured away from her war party. Her sorry state had been accrued over several days of meetings and light torture. Something though... something was different today. There was a defiance in her eyes that had not been there in previous days. The party leader did not appreciate the shift. "Filthy *human*, the only thing waiting for you in the testing zones is death. I only hope my clan is the one to find you after your inevitable respawn."

After speaking these words, she released a hideous snarl and lunged for the human's throat. Unfortunately for her, as soon as she began moving toward the Rogue, his dagger pierced her heart three times. If her expression weren't so gleeful as she collapsed, the man was sure he would have been fine with witnessing her death. He spit on the furry corpse, giving it a kick for good measure. "What a waste. Ladies and gentlemen, it looks like we are going to find our little runaway the old-fashioned way. Be ready for anything."

JAXON

The third open room was similar to the first two, the only real difference being the type and number of enemies available. Twenty-five duck sized horses shrieked a high-pitched whinny and stampeded toward him. Jaxon had a minor ethical dilemma; did he feel terrible about punching tiny ponies? When the first of them reared up and kicked with a sharp metal hoof, he realized that he had very few qualms about attacking such adorable foes. He was worried that later in the temple there would be a horse-sized duck, but that was an issue for a later time.

Realistically, they were not an overly difficult enemy to defeat for someone with his levels of strength and dexterity. More than anything, he wanted to hitch them all to a cart and have the cutest mode of transportation in the game. Unfortunately, that option was not available to him. Instead, he reached down and did his very best to snap their necks as quickly and painlessly as possible. A few of them he stomped on, being mindful that the durability of his boots was getting extremely low. He was able to use the extendable needle of his glove on a few of them to great effect, the length of the needle being longer than the distance from the surface of their skin to the brain.

Besides the initial attack on his body, he had not taken any wounds from these creatures by the time they were all defeated. They simply did not have the natural weapons, size, speed, or strength to even land a blow. Jaxon was fairly certain that this was supposed to be more of a blow to the morale of the Challenger than an actual challenge. He left the room without expecting to gain a record but also hoping he wasn't the slowest to have gone through here.

Exp: 100 (4 * Tiny Horse x25).

Congratulations, Challenger! You have set the record for most brutal massacre in the third solo survival room. Others have done it faster, but not many people used a tiny horse to beat another horse to death. Rarity of final reward increased by 5% for completing the room with a record.

Jaxon thought that he was beginning to see a pattern for the amount of enemies and experience he would gain. He went to move on and collapsed to the floor. "What the... oh... hunger and thirst debuff at maximum..."

He gulped, really *feeling* the dry throat, and looked at the bodies of the tiny horses next to him. Jaxon tried not to think about it, but his stamina was no longer regenerating... he pulled one of the horses closer and used his needle to open a small hole. He bit down and chewed, trying to talk himself through the process. "It's sushi, just really *moist* sushi. That helps with the... with the *thirst* too..."

He ate a good portion of two of the small beasts before his stamina was returning normally. Jaxon would normally worry about getting sick later, but he doubted he would survive long enough to get into gastrointestinal distress. Moving into the next room, the fourth room, showed that from here things would not be so simple. There were ten people in this room besides Jaxon, and it was obvious that these were non-player characters. If anything, these were peasants, militia at best. When Jaxon walked into the room covered in blood, gore, looking and possibly smelling like death incarnate... the people in the room became terrified.

"P-please, sir! *Please* don't hurt us!" The first person to speak just *had* to say words that would make Jaxon hesitate. Unfortunately for the terrified serf, this was a trial, and Jaxon had no intention of failing to progress. The Monk ran at the nearest human, fist cocked back and prepared to swing. His blow came down hard, and at the last second, Jaxon barely stopped himself from following through. He looked down, noticing a wet stain spreading across the man's pant leg. Jaxon took a calming breath and walked across the room through the small crowd of people, who, in turn, shied away as he came near them.

He laid his hand on the door leading to the next room, hoping that he had gauged this test correctly. Jaxon pushed, and the door leading to the next room opened. He released a sigh of relief before turning back to the others with a wide smile, "Thank goodness. I am very pleased that I did not need to murder you all in cold blood. That would have certainly reduced my enjoyment of this process."

Stepping into the fifth room, he was spared the sight of matching stains traveling down the pants of every other person in the room.

Congratulations, Challenger! You have set a 'Pacifist' record by passing through the fourth solo survival room without giving or taking a single blow. Rarity of final reward increased by 5% for completing the room with a record. Rarity has reached a minimum of 'Rare'.

Skill increase: Intimidation (Journeyman IV).

"What a *silly* skill!" Jaxon shook his head with a chuckle, sobering quickly as he saw what awaited him in this room. Primates, monkeys similar to the version surrounding the temple, came charging at him as soon as they noticed his intrusion. There would be no peaceful resolution this time, but Jaxon was almost thankful for the opportunity to fight an enemy he understood.

The monkeys were thankfully unable to use their stealth capabilities, and in a straight-up fight, Jaxon could overpower one of them easily; the problem was that there were around a dozen moving toward him at the same time. Jaxon settled down, centering himself and joyfully joining combat. Monkeys, especially of this size, are typically much stronger and more agile than a human. However, thanks to his incredible stat increases, Jaxon was able to fend off the first few blows and put his back to a wall.

Now that he did not need to worry about one direction, he was able to fully focus in front of himself and dedicate himself to battle. He ducked, and four claws tossed out sparks as they made parallel grooves in the wall. As the arm passed over his head, Jaxon drove stiffened fingers into the animal's armpit. The limb was rendered useless and simply dangled at the monkey's side. Jaxon grabbed the uncontrolled arm and swung the beast into another that was jumping at him. They both landed in a jumble, and Jaxon used the opportunity to drive his hands deeply into the neck muscle of another who stumbled over them. With a pinched nerve, that creature fell to the floor in agony.

"Three down momentarily, how to capitalize on this?" Jaxon muttered to himself as howling balls of rage closed in. Seeing no other option, he dove into the scrum and began dealing as much focused damage as possible. Surrounded on all sides, it actually became harder for the monkeys to attack using their typically wild blows. When they tried, they damaged their own comrades at least as often as the human. Thanks to his quick thinking, Jaxon was swiftly able to whittle down their numbers.

When there were four remaining, Jaxon was able to practice his adjustments and acupressure to great effect. He twisted bones, misaligned vertebrae, poked holes in tendons and muscles, and essentially had fun with the process. As the last primates fell, Jaxon found that he was down to a quarter health. He grabbed one of the fallen and used its fur as a mop, possibly as a squeegee, to clear the floor of any liquid that he may accidentally sit in. Then he settled in the area and, after weighing the cost and benefits, decided against using one of the warmer bodies as a pillow. He had not encountered lice or fleas in the game, but that did not mean they didn't exist.

Congratulations Challenger! You have passed through the fifth solo survival room. Rarity of final reward increased by 1% for completing the room without a record.

Jaxon's vision returned quickly as he woke up, and the first thing he saw was the burning eyeball floating in the air above him. As soon as it realized that it had been noticed, it vanished with a slight *pop*. The Monk stood and stretched, ruminating over the fact that he had once again slept on a hard, stone floor. This was not the best way to maintain health, but realistically, he had no choice. As prepared as he could be, Jaxon opened the door to the sixth room and stepped in.

There were only ten enemies here, but watching them was a confusing sight. This was some form of connected group, with each of the creatures wearing a manacle on one ankle that was connected by a chain to each of the others. They were some form of demi-human, specifically a humanoid cat. With Wolfmen being the main opponent for Humanity, other types of demi-human were distrusted and rarely seen. Retractable claws popped out of their paws, and they moved together as a unit to charge at him.

No matter how well-trained or coordinated they were, they got in each other's way. They had also spread out so that Jaxon was not able to leave them alone and go toward the exit door. Obviously, this was a group of enemies that *wanted* to fight. Jaxon used a few precious moments to study their physical structure, confirming that they had similar enough anatomy for his skills to be useful against them. Just before he began his assault, one of them spoke to him.

"Our freedom is at hand!" the Cat Man hissed triumphantly. "The life of a single human in return? Not even a question!"

Jaxon immediately realized that some of the creatures in this place were not here willingly; they were not a test of morality nor were they created by the temple as some form of mindless construct. At the same time, he was unwilling to simply allow them to slay him. Jaxon sidestepped out of range just before an attack that would have flayed him missed by less than an inch. Initially, he kept his hands up to defend himself, but as a set of claws tore into the door and wall behind him, he realized the only way to defend was to dodge. Taking an attack from one of them would be incredibly dangerous, and so he resolved not to be hit. Jaxon's next movement forced him to slam his back into the wall, but he moved forward immediately and drove his fist into the Cat Man's gut.

"I'm going to enjoy slashing you to ribbons," the Cat Man wheezed as he sucked air.

Jaxon had felt the movement of his opponent's ribs as he landed that single blow and realized that their bones must be extremely fragile but were most likely very flexible as well. He cut forward and to the side, shifting his arm out of the way as the other cats attempted to release a flurry of slashing attacks on him. To test his theory, Jaxon put all of his strength behind a single backhand with his gauntlet-clad fist and crushed the skull of the chatty Cat Man.

He was not expecting the air to shudder nor the body to vanish instantaneously. Jaxon nearly lost his balance thanks to his surprise but turned the movement into a forward roll. This allowed him to dodge the dagger-like claws that had attempted to tear his face off, but as he came to his feet, he was forced to dodge again and again. One of their members disappearing had some effect on the others. Whether it was a magical buff that gave them higher speed and dexterity or if it was the simple fact that there was one less person to get in their way; their accuracy, speed, and ability to dodge had increased by a significant margin.

He landed another full-powered strike, and another fell. The third time that Jaxon attempted to do this, the attack was easily dodged. Uh-oh. The creature countered in the opening presented by stepping forward with his hand and tearing a bloody handhold into Jaxon's arm. With his arm being gripped, Jaxon's ability to dodge or roll away was severely impacted. Luckily for him, the Cat Man holding him was also going to have a hard time getting away from Jaxon. Using his left hand was not ideal, but after three attacks into his opponent's neck, a thin needle punctured its jugular vein. It began taking severe damage-over-time and quickly fell.

When that one vanished with the customary *pop* and the others once again moved faster, Jaxon knew that he might be in trouble.

CHAPTER SEVENTEEN

Jaxon coughed and sprayed a mix of blood and phlegm onto the floor. He was down to three opponents, but each of them was moving so quickly that he was having a hard time keeping up with dodging their attacks, let alone making any of his own. Frankly, he was nervous that defeating any more of them would cause the others to be able to tear him to shreds with ease.

The best-case scenario would be to defeat all of them at the same time with some tricky maneuver, some clever plan, but he had nothing. Joe was the one who could make a sly plan come together; Jaxon was the sort of person who damaged his opponents until they stopped moving. Wait... stop them from moving?

With all the force he could muster, Jaxon activated intimidation. "*Stop right there, criminal scum!*"

He chose those words because they reminded him of a game he had played in the past, where this phrase had been one to inspire fear and an 'oh dang' moment. Just as he had hoped, for a bare second, his powerful intimidation effect caused the three cats to stop and flinch. Using every last drop of his stamina, Jaxon swung with his right hand, his left, and his right again. The first two attacks generated instant death for his targets, but the third and final enemy was so powerfully enhanced that it was able to dodge as if Jaxon were moving in slow motion.

His final opponent's manacle snapped, and the chain that had bound it vanished into motes of light. From that point forward, Jaxon had a hard time following what was happening. Although his dexterity would allow him to dodge every attack if he could see it coming, his perception was simply not up to the task. The demi-human tore open Jaxon's left thigh, then ran to the wall and used it as a springboard to get onto his other side. Razor sharp claws dug into Jaxon's right rib cage, only the bones stopping his lung from being punctured. Jaxon had forty-six health remaining at this point and had no illusions that he would be winning this fight, let alone the next one he would need to face.

Why was he not already dead? His oxygen-starved brain tried to answer the simple question, knowing that it would have significant bearing on this fight. He remembered in the past how he would watch cats play with their kills and realized that was exactly what was happening. The only way to win, or at least to defeat his opponent, was to make the fight no longer *fun*. Jaxon slid to the ground bonelessly, doing his best to play dead. The Cat Man stopped and sighed, as if it was genetically forced to do so, and sauntered over to complete its kill.

It reached down and grabbed Jaxon by the neck, pulling him upright and beginning to squeeze. Jaxon smacked at its wrist uselessly, already fighting for air. This caused a grin to appear on the Cat Man's face, and it let out a slow, pleased chuckle. "That was plenty of fun, but I must say I am pleased that I am the one who gets to exact revenge. Heh-heh. After all... if someone were exacting revenge *for* me, that would mean that I fell in combat. A good fight, for a human."

Jaxon simply smiled as his vision began to fade, so the beastman frowned and began swinging its arm to tear his throat open. Jaxon closed his eyes and activated Adjust. Slapping at the demi-human's arm had kept the needle from extending, but he now had ten stacks of Adjust on the wrist. As the skill activated, Jaxon's opponent was rocked with a hundred points of damage, shattering not only its wrist but the bone all the way to the shoulder.

Taking a deep, heaving breath, Jaxon pulled air into his withered lungs. He stumbled forward, tackling the Cat Man to the ground and landing several weak and sloppy blows on its chest. The monster was fully in shock, its brain dealing with the absolute agony it was in as well as trying to process the adrenaline pumping through it. By the time it could focus enough to launch a counterattack, all it could see was a fist coming for its face.

Exp: 25 (25 * Kitty Kitty Chain Gang x1) (Level seven).

Exp: 30 (30 * Kitty Kitty Chain Gang x1) (Level eight).

This was getting tedious. Jaxon skipped to the final two messages.

Exp: 120 (60 * Kitty Kitty Chain Gang x2) (Level fourteen).

Exp: 70 (70 * Kitty Kitty Chain Gang x1) (Level sixteen).

It seemed that each of the enemies in the room increased by a level each time one of their compatriots died except at the very end, where Jaxon killed two of them nigh simultaneously. Those two had both counted as level fourteens, although the final one had still gone up two levels. Jaxon had gained twenty-five experience plus five experience per level of the demi-human. He was damaged and near death, but defeating ten foes had netted him a whopping *four hundred and seventy* experience!

He was sixty-seven points away from his next level, but looking at the measly eighteen points he had remaining in his health assured him that the next fights were likely going to be too much for him. His clothes were extremely tattered from the sharp claws that had been cutting into him, so he had no shortage of impromptu bandages to bind his wounds. After the bleeding effect was taken care of and he was applying pressure to his rib cage and thigh, he was down to six points of health.

Congratulations, Challenger! You have passed through the sixth solo survival room. Rarity of final reward increased by 1% for completing the room without a record.

Jaxon leaned against the wall, taking deep breaths and trying to calm down. Over the next hour or so, his health slowly regenerated. Unfortunately, his maximum health was capped one hundred and twenty-three points lower than normal due to the grievous nature of his wounds. Until he found a way to be magically healed, surgically healed, or respawned... he was stuck at two hundred and seventy-seven for his maximum health. Typically, this is where Joe would come in and fix him right up. Right now, Jaxon was *really* missing his team leader. Looking at his blinking notifications, he was pleased to see that the fight had at least been beneficial.

Skill increased: Contortionist's Dodge (Student IX).
Skill increased: Intimidation (Journeyman VI).
Skill increased: Aerial Acrobatics (Beginner V).

Three huge skill increases. Woof. He stood up, not tired enough to sleep and knowing that he was losing time. Jaxon looked at the door to the seventh room, acknowledging that it was most likely going to be the final room he entered. He took a deep breath and walked over as confidently as possible. Pushing the door open, he walked in and looked around. Relief filled him; the room was empty! This was obviously some form of resting room, otherwise how would–

A rift appeared in the air in front of his eyes. Not some sort of portal, but it seemed that there was an invisible creature opening its mouth. Jaxon tried to dodge to the side but found that he was surrounded on all sides by the creature's limbs. The appendages tightened, and Jaxon was held in a powerful bear hug as the creature crunched down on his skull.

You have died! Calculating... you lose no experience, but you have been barred from reentry to the Temple of Tempering in the solo areas! Time remaining until respawn... Variable. Reward must be chosen before respawn. Please choose your reward now.

A list grew in front of Jaxon's eyes, seven options only, but how in the world would he be able to choose just *one* of these?

CHAPTER EIGHTEEN

The options were very straightforward, but Jaxon read through them very carefully to ensure that there was no tricky wordplay at work.

Ten free skill points
Five free characteristic points
10,000 experience points
One skill useful to your class (Minimum rarity: Rare)
One weapon designed for your class (Minimum rarity: Rare)
One piece of armor designed for your class (Minimum rarity: Rare)
One accessory designed for your class (Minimum rarity: Rare)

Jaxon was currently in a black space, a void where nothing was around him or visible except for the screen. As interesting as the options were, he was still rather disappointed. Truly, he had hoped that he would find what he needed in order to specialize. Instead, he was looking at a near-standard quest reward. Ah, well. At least he had tried. Jaxon reached out and tapped the skill option.

Are you sure that you want to choose a skill as your reward? You will not be able to change your mind. Yes / No

"Yes, I am sure. Thank you, game, I appreciate you trying to look out for me." Jaxon smiled as the screen in front of him vanished. A spot of color appeared on the horizon, instantly noticeable against the black void. He did not squint; he did not stare. Jaxon knew that if it were coming for him, whatever it was would appear shortly.

Within moments, a massive wheel broken into thousands of tiny segments appeared in front of him. As far as he could see, whether it was up, down, left, or right, the wheel filled his view. The noise of a massive gong being struck filled the area, and a single section of the wheel splintered off. That section shrunk and compressed, turning from a pie slice into its own wheel. That zoomed closer to Jaxon, and all he could see as an identifier was the word 'Monk'.

This tiny wheel began to spin, moving so fast that static electricity built up and discharged around it. With a sound like thunder, it stopped, and Jaxon received a new notification.

Skill gained: Body Compression (Novice IX). Your body is still only flesh and bone, but now it will grow stronger as you deal or receive damage. Gain one health point per five hundred points of damage taken and survived. (Not retroactive). Gain one point of Constitution per 1,000 points of damage dealt from physical attacks. (Not retroactive). Bonuses may increase as the ranking of this skill does.

The world around Jaxon begin to appear again, the black of the Void and the colorful wheel vanishing and the white walls of the temple and the muted browns and greens of the plateau and plains around the area appearing. He was excited about his new ability and was very much so looking forward to speaking with Jess and telling her about it. He was also curious what she had received, since it was likely that she would be able to see and defeat the monster that had taken him down.

"Jess? Jess, are you out yet?" He heard a sound from around the corner of the temple and skipped over to say hello. He screeched to a halt and raised his fists in readiness to attack when he saw the small group of people standing over Jess with a knife to the back of her neck.

"Ah! You must be the famous *Jaxon*!" A man in Rogue leathers stepped away and cautiously approached the Monk. "My name is Chris. I am the leader of this small group. I'm not sure what all Jess has told you, but she ran off with some of our guild's tools. We are simply here to reclaim them. I ask that you stay out of the way, and then we will deal with you soon."

"He means he's going to kill you, Jaxon!" Jess screamed from her position on the ground. "Run! Run, you moron!"

"The hick heard me just as well as you did!" Chris stepped over and kicked her in the side of the face. "He obviously knows *better* than to run like you did!"

Jess just spit out a tooth and tried to get as much blood and saliva as possible on Chris's boot. "Jaxon is not exactly known for his mastery of subtle language."

"Fine, we will deal with him first." The Rogue looked over at Jaxon, measuring him up and down. "You don't seem to understand the situation that you are in, and it seems that Jess does not believe you will be *able* to understand. So I'm going to lay this out for you very clearly: give me all the money you have, give me any items you have, and you are free to go."

"Nah." Jaxon took a threatening step forward. He paused as the knife at Jess's neck dipped and drew blood.

"Ah, ah, ah... none of that now." Chris smiled a sneering grin, flicking his tongue over parched lips. " Either you give it to us willingly, or we take it off of your corpse. Take another move that is not exactly what we tell you to do, and she will be sent to respawn before you. Now, if you both do what I tell you to do... I will make sure to go ahead and leave you here, alive. It is not the most hospitable of places, but from what she tells us, if she were to respawn before you... well, the Wolfmen would not be as pleasant as we are."

Jaxon slowed to a halt, for the first time since joining this game genuinely feeling bad for another person. If Jess were slain here, her respawn point would be the Wolfman encampment, and they would kill her over and over until he was able to arrive and save her. If he were to fling himself off the cliff, the intentional death would likely set his respawn time to double or triple the norm. "What do you want?"

"I already told you." Chris smiled and gestured at Jaxon. "I want all the money and items you have. Keep the ratty stuff you're wearing, but lose the gloves. I can recognize a fist fighter when I see one. Don't bother trying to hide things. We can scan your inventory."

Jaxon reached into his inventory and pulled out a small fistful of coins: a couple gold but mostly silver and a single copper. He tossed them to the ground, followed by some seeds, a picture of a skeleton covered by a goopy, red overlay, a few empty bottles, and an empty water jug. Then he took off his gloves and threw them on the pile, finally looking up and staring at the thieves. "All set then?"

"Sure looks like it." Chris took the money, the water jug, and the gloves. After he picked over the pile, he turned back to the others. "This guy is carrying around more trash than *anything* actually useful. He has more *seeds* than coins on him! You planning to be a farmer, Jaxon?"

His party members laughed along with him and moved away from Jess. She slowly sat up, apparently exhausted by the whole ordeal. Chris walked over to her, grabbed her by the chin, and forced her to meet his eyes. "You find and return that dagger. You try to skip out on this, and we'll hunt you until you hit level one again. You get me?"

Jess averted her eyes, so Chris smacked her in the face. "I said, *get* me?"

"I get you, Chris! Jeez!" Jess spat out a mouthful of blood from the powerful backhand.

"Well, hot dang, she can listen." Chris strode over to his team and started down the plateau without looking back. "Let's get going. Looks like we need to try and recruit a new member again. Have fun with those monkeys, you two!"

After Jaxon and Jess were alone again, Jaxon blew out an extended breath. "Fun friends you have, there. I'm glad I took a *skill* reward."

"You had the option for a skill reward?" Jess looked up, her curiosity beating out her anger and embarrassment momentarily. "How far did you get through the temple?"

"I only got to the seventh room. There was some kind of invisible monster that bit my head off." Jaxon growled about that, but there was no help for it at this point. "How about yourself?"

"Room three," she stated quietly. "It was really hard to do anything without a weapon. Listen, Jaxon, I'm so sorry. I'll find a way to make it up to you."

"Don't you worry your pretty little head about that. Some people are just terrible for no good reason. We didn't lose anything that is hard to replace, so how about we just figure out what to do next?" Jaxon offered his hand to her and pulled her off the ground. As he did so, a door appeared and opened in the wall. "What the...?"

He let go of her hand, and the door vanished as if it had never existed. Grabbing her hand again, the doorway opened. "You know... I do remember this place telling me that I was only barred from *solo* attempts. Want to go together?"

Jess was staring at the temple with burning fervor. "Oh, *abyss* yes."

CHAPTER NINETEEN

"Before we go in, we should really go over a few things." Jaxon let go of Jess's hand and sat down. "Should I be concerned about those people? Are they going to come back? How can we work best as a team?"

"They got what they wanted, and their cruelty is only matched by their laziness." Jess spat to the side, disgusted with them and the fact that she had been trying so hard to *join* them. "They won't be back. As for how I can help in there, unless I get some kind of dagger, I am only going to be useful for tactics and spotting enemies. I think that is your weakness, so at least I can make up for that."

"I see. Yes, that would be nice. I will be able to help by beating our opponents to death." Jaxon smiled brightly as he spoke. "To me, not having a hand-covering weapon means that I will need to paint the enemies in my blood as I fight. Perhaps I can make a rudimentary hand wrap with the scraps I was using to bind my open wounds a little while ago."

"You are so *strange*, Jaxon." Jess shook her head in frustration. "I have no idea where you get this attitude. It's really out of place."

"Jess, I wasn't joking a while back. I'm in my nineties in real life. I spent my entire life attempting to master and perfect my chiropractic abilities and built an empire devoted to health and healing. I... I may have been *too* focused in the past because it was over five years before I found out that I had been voted out of my own company by the board of directors. I was given a pension and a cold 'thank you for your time'. Then I had no family, friends, or coworkers. I became even more obsessed with perfecting my craft."

"If you are so down about that, why are you still trying to work as a chiropractor here?" Jess candidly questioned him.

"What are you talking about?" Jaxon cocked his head to the side like a dog hearing the word 'treat'.

"Well, you still seem obsessed with your work. If it brought you so much heartache, why not find something else to do?" Jess trailed off as she saw him shaking his head.

"You misunderstand." Jaxon threw his arms to the side and stared at the sky in wonder. "Thanks to this game, someday I can *objectively* and *empirically* claim that I have learned everything there is to know! I have the body of my youth back and have strength and a range of movement I never expected! *Everything* else is secondary to becoming the ninth-level Sage of Chiropractic Care! I'm not *sad* about my past. Everything has led me to the here and now!"

Still staring up with his arms splayed and chest heaving with excitement, Jaxon had never looked more insane to Jess. She coughed, and he seemed to realize that something was amiss. "Eherm. Tell me... um. Tell me about you?"

She snorted and rolled her eyes. "Not that you care about anything but work, obviously, but I'm thirty, unemployed, and getting *deeper* in debt so that I can try and make money in this game. I'm in a pod, like any serious player, but the upkeep is ruining me. I used to play games super seriously when I was younger, and I've always been really good at setting up raids and player vs player stuff. I'm a strategist and tactician before anything else."

Jaxon pondered her words for a few moments. "Are you opposed to being a party planner? An agent of sorts, someone who plans that stuff out for groups?"

"If it pays better than what I've been trying to do, I'd go for it." Jess eyed Jaxon, a spark of hope lighting her gaze up.

"Please tell me there is an offer or something at the end of this questioning."

"Sort of." Jaxon nodded and stood up. "My party is the squad called in by the guild when standard tactics won't work out, and we are pretty good at being reactionary. We don't really have any direction, though, and only *reacting* isn't enough. If you wanted, I'm pretty sure I could get you a position as our Operations Expert. Set up things for us to do, manage our schedules, tell us what we will need to get through an already explored area, and other stuff like that."

"What does it pay? Don't get me wrong, I'm interested, but I have debts," Jess hedged.

"I'm sure we can work something out." Jaxon offered her a hand up. She took it and stood with him while the temple door opened once more. "Now, this will likely be harder, especially since you are weaponless, but let's get in there and win amazing rewards!"

They stepped into the temple together, and the floor fell out from under them. Jess screamed in surprise, but Jaxon simply laughed and enjoyed the ride. It didn't occur to him till they landed and slid across the floor that she had been able to walk into the place normally before. Maybe he was the reason the floor kept dropping out? Jaxon shot to his feet and looked around excitedly, hoping that there would be a swarm of skeletons he could play with again. Once again, he saw a flaming eyeball appear right before a screen covered his vision.

Welcome Challengers! You have entered the Temple of Tempering! By reaching this location, you have passed the first test. From this point forward, the longer you survive, the greater your rewards will be. When you both die, you will be placed in front of the temple and barred from reentering the duo halls. If one of you manages to survive after the other falls, you will be returned to the room with your maximum health halved if the area is completed. Do your best, for you will not have another chance. The countdown to your death begins... now!

No skeletons were rushing him, no humanoid enemies were around at all. There were ferns filling the room, but otherwise, there was nothing standing between them and the exit. Jess piped up, "Do you think there are monsters hiding in the shrubs?"

"We'll find out, I guess." Jaxon strode toward the door, parting the bushes with his confident walk. Jess followed close behind, but they reached the door without incident. "Just... leave, I guess? At least we should get the pacifist award."

"The what?"

Jaxon opened the door without answering, instantly confused at the message that popped up.

Congratulations, Challenger! Rarity of final reward increased by 1% for completing the first duo survival room without a record.

"Why didn't we get an award for not taking or giving any hits?" Jaxon muttered aloud while pulling open his combat log.

Awakened Shrub attacks with special ability 'Terrain Damage'. Hp -0.

...

Awakened Shrub attacks with special ability 'Terrain Damage'. Hp -0.

Jaxon looked over the list containing *hundreds* of attacks against them and looked back at the room in a new light. The shrubs hadn't damaged them, but what were those things going to grow into? He took a step back and reached for one of the plants, only stopping himself from harvesting it at the last second.

That... that would be an attempt at using a Herbalism skill, wouldn't it? That could mess with his potential rewards...

"What are you doing, Jaxon?" Jess impatiently was trying to peer into the next room, but there was a thin layer of darkness that clung to the opening and didn't allow for planning.

"Nothing... I suppose." He returned to her, and they stepped through to the next room together.

Caw! Caw! Caw!

A murder of crows was flying around this room and began dive-bombing the duo as they walked into the room. The first one swiped at Jaxon, getting a fist to the chest for its trouble. It exploded in a spray of blood, notably not even leaving feathers behind. Jaxon had a bad feeling and tried to tell Jess to stay back. *"Stand behind me, small and frail person!"*

Whoops, that came out weird. Jaxon decided it was close enough to what he wanted to say, so he began punching the crows as they came near.

Status change: Toxic Blood. Your blood is rotting in your body. -2% maximum health per ten seconds. If you die while under this ailment, your body will be used to generate Blood Borne Crows. Time remaining: 12:00... 11:59...

Thank goodness! At first, he had thought he had a twelve-hour ailment. The crows were swooping at Jess, obviously trying to either infect her with an attack or get her to touch them. Either of these would get them the results they were hoping for. Jaxon charged over and took a beak that would have speared her from behind, eliminating the crow by grabbing it and crushing it against the wall. A puddle of blood formed on the wall and dripped down, but Jaxon had already turned his attention to the others. They were incredibly fragile, but he found that their infection stacked.

Status change: Toxic Blood. Your blood is rotting in your body. -6% maximum health per ten seconds. If you die while under this ailment, your body will be used to generate Blood Borne Crows. Time remaining: 12:00... 11:59...

Drat, it also reset the timer. He was going to die from this for *sure*. He needed to clean up the remainder before he went down, or Jess would die as well. As the birds swooped down, he recklessly took every hit and doled out a single fist to each of them. The final one exploded into a bloody mist, and Jaxon looked at the counter. 28% health per second. "Good-bye, Jess. See you in a moment."

Exp: 68 (4 * Blood Borne Crow x17).

Congratulations, Challenger! You have set the record for highest amount of status-impairing effects in room number two! Rarity of final reward increased by 5% for completing the second duo survival room with a record.

You have leveled up! You have reached character level 12! You currently have three free Characteristic points to spend and twelve skill points!

Jaxon was lifted off the floor, and a blast of golden light washed out from him, cleaning the area and removing his illness. He settled back down on the floor and sat down. "Way... too... close..."

Not wanting to wait, he opened up his status screen and added in the characteristic points he had just gained. All three went to Constitution, since he had been taking far too many hits recently. Also, he had been noticing that his intense movements had been causing him pain as his body hit its limit. His hope was that balancing his Con would help fix that issue.

Name: Jaxon 'Legend' Class: Monk
Profession: Chiropractor

Level: 12 Exp: 78,001 Exp to next level: 12,999
Hit Points: 126/430 (50+(380)) (Base 50 plus 10 points for each point in Constitution, once it has increased above 10.)
Mana: Locked
Mana regen: Locked
Stamina: 200/555 (50+(315)+(190)) (Base 50 plus 5 points for each point in strength and constitution, once each of the stats has increased above 10.)

Characteristic: Raw score (Modifier)

Strength: 73 (2.21)
Dexterity: 100 (3.0)
Constitution: 48 (1.48)
Intelligence: 26 (1.26)
Wisdom: 35 (1.35)
Charisma: 5 (0.05)
Perception: 21 (1.21)
Luck: 44 (1.44)
Karmic Luck: 0

Exhausted and near death, Jaxon laid on the floor and chatted with Jess for a bit as they waited for his health to refill. Since he didn't have any wounds, Jaxon's health returned to its maximum. He stood, nodded, and they stepped into the third room.

CHAPTER TWENTY

When Jaxon stepped through the door and saw what was waiting for them, he instantly tried to turn around and go back. That didn't work; the dark film over the door preventing retreating. Jess stepped through and grimaced at their foes, nodding at his reaction. "Oh, ew. Good call. Let's try not to let them touch us if possible."

Jaxon blinked at her and looked back at the fluffy kittens slowly and cautiously coming toward them. "Your reaction confuses me."

"Well, I mean... I'm not a huge fan of touching those things, but I feel like I could take most of them out even if I were alone, so this should be pretty easy with the two of us."

"Jess, I can't kill those! I would never be able to forgive myself! They are *far* too cute," Jaxon sputtered as she rolled her eyes at him.

"Sheesh, I knew you were into weird stuff, why am I not surprised that *this* is what would get you squeamish? Fine, I'll take care of it," she muttered to herself as she moved towards the cats, only stopping after she had crushed the first under her boot. "They *are* hostile, Jaxon! We can't get to the door without doing this!"

"I... I can't even begin to..." Jaxon watched in horror as body after body was crushed or smacked away by Jess. He didn't lift a finger to help her, simply gaping until she had finished them all off.

"Jaxon! What the heck, man?" Jess snarled as she stalked over to him. "I had to kill, like... three dozen rats by myself!"

"*Rats?* You were stomping on *kittens!*" Jaxon almost gagged as he spoke. Jess smacked him lightly across the face to snap him out of it.

"I did *not!* My combat log says I just killed thirty-six 'tiny beasts'. There must be some mind-altering stuff going on here."

Congratulations, Challengers! You have set the speed record for the third duo survival room! Rarity of final reward increased by 5% for completing the third duo survival room with a record.

"I bet there is something that made those rats super cute to everyone who came through here. I'm glad my perception is high enough to ignore it, or we would've never set that record." Jess smugly strutted toward the door, Jaxon trailing behind with an uncomfortable expression on his face.

They entered the fourth room with a grimace, knowing that it would be much harder to win than the previous room was. At least, that was the assumption. Jaxon had to reevaluate his thoughts toward this dungeon when he saw several large sharks thrashing around on the floor. They were already starting to suffocate, but the fact that they weren't already dead told Jaxon that their opponent was added to the room right as the challenger entered. While this was an interesting development, it didn't stop him from charging forward and landing a hefty punch on each of the sharks.

"Jaxon! What are you doing?"

"Getting experience!" Jaxon looked back at her with a bloodthirsty grin. "These things are *huge* and, I'm betting, high level. Not my fault that they can't breathe, but I see no need to be wasteful."

Jess didn't even wait for the explanation to be complete before she was attacking the sharks as well. Their rubbery hide didn't sustain much damage, and frankly, the blunt attacks they were able to make with their bare hands wouldn't allow for any lasting damage to any part of the predators. None of that mattered though, because in a few minutes all of the sharks had suffocated.

Congratulations Challengers! You have attained a 'David and Goliath' record for defeating enemies more than double your level in the fourth duo survival room! Rarity of final reward increased by 85% for completing the fourth duo survival room with a record. Minimum reward rarity set to Rare.

Exp: 360 (1,800 * Giant Shark x4 * .05 Kill Contribution).

"Good lord, those things were worth nearly two thousand experience each?" Jaxon smiled happily as he reached for the sharks, ready to tear them open and learn about them but stopped just before he touched the rough surface.

Jess had been watching him the whole time, and she had seen him do something similar with the plants in the first room. "Alright, I need to know what the heck is going on here. You keep wanting to do something, then holding back. Are you wanting to eat them or something? Are you worried that I will lose respect for you or something? I don't think it's possible, so don't worry about that."

"Oh, that's very sweet of you! I didn't realize that I rated so highly in your mind." Jaxon kept speaking even as Jess tried to interrupt him for some reason, "No, I was told that completing the temple using only skills for your class or ones you want to enhance was the best way to go. Anything else could make the rewards offered vary wildly, so I am being careful not to accidentally use some kind of harvesting skill."

Jess looked thoughtful, nodding slowly in realization. "That at least explains my last run through. One of my reward options was an occupation change... alright. Let's get through the rest of this place as fast as possible."

As they walked toward the next room, Jaxon blinked a few times. "Why the rush? There isn't a time limit as far as I could tell."

"Yeah, actually, why *did* it take so long for you to get out of there the first time? I was on the ground for two hours as we waited for you."

"I took a nap between most of the battles. I was trying to get a meditative skill or something that would be useful for my personal recovery." Jaxon tossed his hands into the air in frustration. "It seems I cannot make it work for me, no matter what I try."

"You were taking *naps*?" Jess seemed stuck on that point, and Jaxon felt that there would have been an argument or something if they didn't walk into the next room at that exact moment. "My face was being pushed into the ground for *hours* and you were taking n–"

"Whoa. Those guys are *big and ugly*," Jaxon spoke the words before he could stop himself and had to wonder where all of his self-control had gone. He looked at what was waiting for them once again and shrugged. At least he hadn't lied, and it seemed that Jess was firmly distracted.

"No *way*. Those are straight out of mythos! Those are *Lemure*! They are a type of animalistic demon that rely on strength and clubs to destroy their opponents!" Jess was geeking out pretty hard, so Jaxon spoke up to remind her of the situation.

"I thought lemurs were small monkeys? Listen, I'm glad you are excited, but... *we* are their opponent here, right? Any weaknesses that you remember?" Jaxon's words had the same effect a pin had on a balloon. She deflated visibly and attempted to remember anything that would help them.

"No, unless you have holy magic, we are going to have to beat them to death or try to get out of here as soon as possible." Jess was leaning toward the second option, that much was obvious. It didn't look like they were going to get a chance to debate and make a choice; the demonic beings were charging at them with looks of malicious glee.

Jaxon darted forward and met their headlong rush with his own, slipping around the massive beings with timely uses of his dodging skill. The solid stone floor shattered wherever their weapons hit, even with the lightest of strikes. Jaxon knew for sure that if he were to take even a glancing impact, the result would be his death, if not from the first hit, then from the *next* one when he was on the floor gasping in pain from all the broken bones.

Wham

Jaxon dodged the attack, but the shattering ground sent shards of stone into his face, and he flinched away. He tried to do a backflip to get away from whatever attack would be coming next, but he was hit by a club and sent sailing like a home run. The wall came closer, closer... then everything went black.

Momentarily.

You have died! Calculating... you lose no experience. Time remaining until respawn... Variable.

Your partner has completed the survival room! You will appear in the room with your health capped 50% lower. Arriving in 3... 2... 1...

Jaxon came back to life shouting, "*Ow!* That *hurt,* and how on earth did you win? I'm not doubting your competence, only your odds of survival."

"You are *welcome.* I didn't fight them. I ran for the exit while you kept them busy. Sorry you had to die for it, but if it makes you feel any better, we got another five percent on our reward rarity for setting a speed record."

"That actually does help me feel better, thank you." Jaxon looked around, trying to gauge what the threat level they would face here could be. "Do we have invisible enemies?"

"No, just tiny ones." Jess pointed at the floor, and Jaxon leaned down to get a better look. "Snakes. I'm assuming poisonous ones since there are so few and they are so small."

"How many in total?"

"Nine. At least that I can find. So be careful where you step," Jess pointedly ordered him.

"Jess, let's be serious here. I only saw *this* one because you specifically pointed it out for me." Jaxon stood straight again and cracked his neck. Tell me where to walk, and I'll take care of the snakes. I freakin' love snakes."

He took a step toward the snake that had been pointed out, moving his arms in undulating patterns as he moved. The snake got into a tiny coil and stared at him, flicking its tongue uncertainly. Jess shoved Jaxon forward, and a nearly invisible snake arced through the air where he had just been standing. The snake Jaxon had been focusing on saw this as an attack and used its coiled position to launch into the air at the human's face. Jaxon caught the tiny reptile gently, sending it to the other side of the room with a flick of his fingers so it couldn't bite him.

"Let's hurry through here. I don't want these perfect specimens of healthy spinal columns to accidentally get hurt." Jaxon moved to the left just as another snake passed his neck.

Luck +1.

"Can I *intentionally* hurt them?" Jess grumped at him. "Seriously, I don't know what is going on with this place. It either gives us enemies we don't want to hurt, *can't* hurt, or can destroy way too easily. Why not something that is a *fair* fight? *Ouch!*"

Jaxon looked back and saw a tiny snake thrashing around, having locked onto her throat. Foam flecked her lips as she spoke the last words she could manage before dropping to her knees, "*Jaxon*. Run!"

She spasmed once more and fully collapsed. Jaxon wasted no more time flipping backward and skipping at full speed to the exit. His sporadically swinging body made the surprisingly speedy snakes miss their subsequent series of strikes. Jaxon shoved open the door and slid through.

Congratulations, Challengers! You have attained a 'Beneficent Human' record for not killing your opponents, even while you easily could have killed them without taking damage. Sixth duo survival room completed! Rarity of final reward increased by 20% for completing the sixth duo room with a record. Minimum reward rarity set to Unique.

"Nice!" Jaxon told Jess the happy news as she appeared next to him. Then he looked around the room, and his smile faded a little. "Well, Jess, I think we had a good run."

"What are you..." Her face paled as she took in the opponents arrayed against them. Six... *creatures* were staring at them through beady eyes nearly hidden by their shells. They were heavily naturally-armored quadrupeds, somewhat lizard-like, with their heads making up two-thirds of their total size. One of them opened their mouth and opened and opened it. Its jaw was open wide enough to engulf Jaxon with a single chomp, and he wanted no part of that action. There had to be magic involved for these things to exist, otherwise they would simply topple over due to their unbalanced bodies.

The massive beast in the lead moved back a bit, then launched forward at a speed that should have been impossible, somehow leaping with its heavy body nearly a dozen feet toward them. It landed as the humans tried to dodge, catching them off-guard and bowling them over. The others jumped and landed, forming a massive dogpile that crushed both humans to death.

You have died! Calculating... you lose no experience, but you have been barred from reentry to the Temple of Tempering in the solo and duo areas! Time remaining until respawn... Variable. Reward must be chosen before respawn. Please choose your reward now.

CHAPTER TWENTY-ONE

"So we have to choose something to share between us?" Jess's voice caused Jaxon to scream, a long and shrill sound that only slowly petered off.

He caught his breath, turning and looking at the incorporeal form of the woman standing beside him. "Oh. Jess. You startled me."

"No crap." Jess was eying him up and down as if he were suddenly going to sprout a second head devoted to screaming. "What do you think we should get?"

Jaxon turned back to the rewards, and they started going through the options together. As they discussed the available Unique rewards, there was one obvious problem. Jaxon was the first to vocalize the issue, but Jess nodded along grimly to his words, "It appears that there is a great reward in the form of two-piece set items, but if we split them up, they become little better than trash. Everything else is... *okay*, but these are the obvious rewards to take."

"So now the question becomes: how do we decide who gets the set item, or do we settle for subpar rewards?" Jess finished the line of thought for the both of them, and they both settled into introspective silence.

"I think–" Jaxon started.

"I don't mind–" Jess spoke at the same time, stopping herself from completing the sentence when she realized they were talking over each other. "Go ahead."

"Sure. I think that this place is really designed for people that have been together a long time or really trust each other. It's obvious that by working together, one person could leave here *much* stronger than when they walked in, but that means there is going to need to be a lot of trust involved."

"I don't mind taking a lesser reward. That way we both get something for sure." Jess sighed and motioned at the consumables, money, or experience options that had appeared.

"Nah. Even with how cool some of these items look, they don't really fit into what I want to be doing. Let's get one of the set items, and you can have it." Jaxon shrugged as Jess looked at him skeptically.

"How do I know that you aren't just trying to screw me out of a reward?" Her voice was dark; obviously, she had gone through some trouble in her past.

"Call it an introductory offer from my party. This way you can start working with us *knowing* that we operate in good faith." Jaxon's smile seemed to take on a different light to Jess. No longer was he incredibly menacing; he was simply... *very* intimidating.

"Alright then." Jess swallowed and looked at the studded leather armor that had made her heart sing. "I really want this set."

Jaxon looked it over and nodded. "A flat five percent increase to dexterity, a scaling defense ability, limited self-repair, a once a day 'flash step', and a ten percent bonus to stealth. Probably because it is made out of *hide*, huh? *Huh?*"

"Oh my *gosh*," Jess groaned with an eye roll. "You are the absolute *worst*. Can we get this then?"

"You're sure?" Jess nodded at him, so Jaxon finalized the selection. A pair of studded leather leggings appeared in his hands and a similarly designed chest piece in hers. He handed over the item before she could become worried in the slightest and then vanished from Jess's view as she respawned in front of the temple.

"Jaxon?" She looked around but didn't see the man. Shrugging, she put on the armor and began testing out her new capabilities.

The Monk was having a very different experience. Jess had vanished from his awareness, and the void around him was now shining with golden light.

Congratulations, Jaxon! You have passed the duo trial! By fully giving the reward to your companion without expectation of rewards for yourself, you have proven that you are trustworthy and generous. These are the most important traits in any long-term relationship. While this knowledge about yourself should be reward enough, passing the trial demands compensation. Scanning... accessing skills. Accessing desires. Accessing quests. Accessing titles.

Possible reward determined: Unique Specialization. Requirements: 'Monk' class. A title that allows you to interact with specific animals (Title: 'Snake Charmer' selected, Title: 'Entomologist' can be selected for usage instead). A powerful Monk-specific title (Title: 'Legend' is valid substitute). Total cost reduced by half thanks to 'duo success' modifier. Cost: Five ranks of 'Acupressure' skill. Five ranks of 'Adjust' skill. Ten ranks of 'Contortionist's Dodge' skill. Eight ranks of 'Body Compression' skill.

There are no current trainers for the specialization offered, and no further information can be offered without accepting the class. Accept? Yes / No.

Jaxon's finger hovered over the 'accept' button, but he was having a hard time with the thought of giving up two Master level skills. Also, his dodge skill did more than just help him dodge; it helped his body *bend* in ways it normally couldn't. He had never heard of a specialization costing like this! Why was he being charged just to rank up? Then again... he would be blazing a trail for others to follow, and he was sure the rewards for this choice would *eventually* pay dividends. Not allowing himself to mourn the loss, he mashed the 'Yes' button twice, not giving himself a chance to be talked out of it.

He screeched as he felt some of his memories vanish. An entire section of how to properly treat his patients was just *gone*. He knew it even if he couldn't remember exactly what those methods were or how to pursue and reclaim them. His body stiffened slightly, then *more* than slightly. Ten percent less ability to bend was a serious inconvenience. Jaxon *really* hoped this reward would be worth the loss. Body Compression was less of a loss, even though it would have been useful to start that at a higher level.

Assigning reward. Congratulations! you have earned the specialized class: Bonecruncher (Mythical). Class bonuses: Gain +3 Dexterity, Strength, and Luck every even class level! Lose 1 Charisma each third class level. Gain the class skill: Living Weapon. To increase your class level, defeat opponents using your class skill.

Your Mana has been unlocked!

Skill gained: Living Weapon (Novice I). Your hands now have the ability to transform into living weapons which will have their own damage, statistics, and levels. Caution! Your weapons have been designated as a creature in the same phylum as the creature title used in class generation. You will need to teach, train, and control your living weapons in order to use them properly. Current cost: 50 mana per second. Length of transformation is dependent upon class level, weapon level, and how well-trained your weapons are. Cooldown: 30 minutes.

Caution! It is recommended that you do not assign skill points to living weapons until you are certain they are trained.

Jaxon appeared in front of Jess as she was settling back to wait, a sheen of sweat on her face the only sign that she had spent the interim with training instead of lazing around. She was taken aback by his sudden appearance, but easily kept her composure. "Hi, Jaxon. Anything interesting happen since we last talked?"

"I'm pretty sure." There was another notification waiting for his viewing pleasure, but he ignored it for now. Jaxon felt at himself, squeezing his hands and wincing at their reduced mobility. He made a few extra movements, working his way through his normal warm-up exercises. "Ugh. I'm going to really need to work to get those skills back to an acceptable level."

"You lost skill levels?" Jess shot to her feet, looking him over. "What happened? Did you go through another trial or something?"

"No, nothing like that. I got a bonus reward for letting you take all the loot and earned a specialization." He held up a hand as her face brightened and her mouth opened to ask a question. "I lost a whole bunch of skill points, and even though the cost was halved as a reward, it really hurt my abilities. I'm not even sure what happened, and I only got a single skill out of the deal. It's started at Novice *one*, for goodness sake."

"What does it do?" Jess asked quietly, realizing that Jaxon was having a hard time right now.

"I have no idea. It seems to make my hands deadlier as weapons or something." Jaxon lifted his bare hands, not even needing to inspect them to know that there was no change. "It's an active skill, so I need to test it out. There aren't any enemies around, though, so I'm not sure whether I should bother."

"Do you need to have a target?"

Jess's question made Jaxon pause. "No. No, I suppose I don't, do I? Good idea. Let's see what happens. I can only hold the transformation for six seconds at a maximum right now anyway."

Keeping his hands held high, he spoke the skill aloud and with authority, "*Living Weapons.*"

His hands spasmed, and his fingers locked together. They shifted and *compressed*, bending forward as if he were reaching for his elbows with his fingertips. There was a small surge of *strangeness*, neither light nor sound but something that hurt the mind to look at directly. The change was actually nearly instantaneous, but as it was the first time he had experienced the shifting sensation, Jaxon was able to experience the change on a visceral level. As the skill finished activating, he looked at what had previously been hands on the end of his arms... and they looked back. With a trumpeting roar, his hands announced to the world that they *lived!*

Jaxon looked over at Jess with maniacal glee showing on his face. "Jess, I take back every complaint I made about this. I have *T-Rex Head Hands!*"

CHAPTER TWENTY-TWO

"Whoa, there! Bad lefty! Down!" Jaxon forcefully pulled his hand away from his face as it snapped at him, saliva splashing on his cheek. He looked over at Jess as he ran out of mana and his hands returned to their normal state. "Whew! My goodness, I haven't had to tame my hands since I went through puberty!"

"Disgusting." Jess sniffed at him. "So... what the heck just happened?"

"I ran out of mana to sustain the T-Rex head hands." Jaxon was squeezing his hands into fists, trying to feel exactly what had changed with the skill usage.

"Not what I meant." Jess was staring at his hands as if she expected them to lunge at her. In other words, no different than usual. "Also, don't call them that! They have a skill name."

"Should I give them names, do you think? I called this guy 'Lefty' out of habit, but as a T-Rex head, should it be something different?" Jaxon was staring with rapt fascination at his hands.

"Your *normal* fists have names?" Jess shook herself, trying to focus on the situation. Jaxon's strangeness seemed to be infecting her. "I meant: what was that? Was that the class skill you got?"

"Yes! Now I need to practice with them and train them. I should really only do that when I have some enemies around. Best way to train something is to have a way to reward it, after all." Jaxon turned on his heel and started walking over to the edge of the plateau the temple was on.

"You're going to *feed* your *hands*?" Jess muttered indignantly, following after him a moment after he dropped off the edge of the cliff. She watched as Jaxon slid down the slope like a snowboarder, somehow maintaining his balance on the steep drop. She shook her head and started carefully making her way down. "If I try that I am going to fall and break something."

Jaxon reached the midpoint of his descent and hopped in the air to shift his momentum a bit. The slope was changing from about seventy degrees to a forty-five-degree angle, so his speed also reduced drastically. His excitement had consequences; his worn-out boots chose this moment to lose their last point of durability and vanished into motes of light with a sound like shattering glass. Jaxon's swift reflexes allowed him to catch his balance, but he was now barefoot on a rocky hill, moving at a fairly high speed. "Ow, oof, *ah!*"

He started to take terrain damage, the rough movement tearing up his feet. Flashes of tiny numbers leaving his health filled his vision, and when he finally got to a flat area, he sat down and gripped his soles as hard as he could and hissed in pain, "*Ssss-ahhhh!*"

Jess slowly made her way down, taking long enough to arrive that Jaxon's health was nearly full. She looked at his position and the blood around his feet, then reached down and pulled a small rock out of his heel. She held up the blood-soaked object and waved it at him. "You can't get to full health with something like this stuck in you. Come on, that's basic."

"I would have gotten around to it." Jaxon looked at his health bar, noting that it had fifteen health greyed out. Drat, unless he got magical healing, a health potion, or some kind of advanced first-aid, his health was capped at four-fifteen. There must have been a bunch of debris or something in his feet as they healed. "Worst possible time for my boots to give out."

"Weren't you crushing small creatures recently by stomping on them? I feel like that would have been worse," Jess retorted with a small, happy smile.

Jaxon was enraptured by the expression and found himself speaking before he could stop himself. "My goodness, you look far less severe and annoying when you smile! It almost makes me forget that you almost murdered me recently."

The first real smile he had seen from her vanished like fog in the noontime sun, and she turned and stalked away from him immediately. Jaxon stood up and reached for her, but she ducked out of his weak grasp. He locked eyes with her. "Jess, I really *mean* that."

"You are *such* an–"

Ah-whooo! The still air was shaken by the throaty howls of the monkeys in the forest. It seemed the humans had been spotted, and the predators in this jungle were *hungry*. Jaxon turned toward the forest and allowed a malicious smile to spread across his lips. "I guess I should get a warm-up in before bringing out Lefty and Terror. Then I can bring them out and show them what happens when you try and attack me. I might even give them a treat if they show the proper respect."

"I can't get over the fact that you are planning to feed your hands." Jess gave up on being mad at Jaxon for now, instead turning to face the loudest of the sounds coming toward them. There were a couple hundred feet of grassy plains surrounding the base of the plateau before the forest began, and though the primates coming toward them were being loud currently, it was unlikely that they would just charge straight at them without even *attempting* a stealth attack.

Sure enough, the howling from the closest group faded away to nothing even as the grass at the edge of the forest started rustling. Jess was easily able to track the progress the animals made, but Jaxon began griping in frustration. "Is the wind moving that section of grass, or is it the stupid monkeys? Are they already behind me?"

Jess grabbed his arm as he started to turn around. "Jaxon, I think one of their skills might be to make you look away from them as they get close so that they take you from behind."

Jaxon's eyes widened in horror. "They can *do* that?"

"What? Of *course* they can stab you in the back." Jess shook her head at Jaxon's oddly relieved expression. "I need you to listen to me. I don't have a weapon, so it'll be really hard for me to fight these things. You can't see them right away, but if we work *together*, I'll be able to let you know where they are and you can fight them off. That sound like a plan?"

"Sounds lovely." Jaxon settled into a fighting stance, then glanced at Jess. "Am... am I facing the right way now?"

"Yup, you're good." Jess stood behind and to the left of him, carefully watching the grass around them. She knew the creatures were close, and she needed to be ready for them. Her eyes caught a faint motion as one of the beasts turned its head too quickly, and she calmly let Jaxon know. "Ahead, just a few feet and to your right. I'm pretty sure that one is the closest to you, and I think it knows it's been seen."

Her warning was spot on, as the Trial Primate chose that moment to act. It exploded out of the grass, which should have been *far* too short to hide this large creature. Jaxon knew it was coming and was even able to dodge most of the swiping claws, but he overestimated his abilities. He had become used to moving and dodging at the last second, but his body was unable to keep up with the strain he put on it with his lowered skill levels. Four lines of blood were drawn on his cheek, passing just under his lips and missing his neck by a hair's length.

Jaxon turned his dodge into an attack of his own, grinding two stiffened fingers into the beast's windpipe and cracking cartilage.

Critical hit! Damage increased by 220% (Acupressure bonus) -66 health!

Jaxon grunted in annoyance as the damage indicator blocked his view—why had it suddenly become an annoyance? Did his preferences get changed? He growled at the notification as he swung his other hand forward. "I can't stand the sight of you. You're so annoying!"

Jess choked just as she was calling out the next attacker, "O-one on your left! Also, *fine!* When this is over, we'll just go our separate ways! Why are you like this?"

"No idea what you mean, Jess." Jaxon punched out, hitting the primate in the thick part of its skull and damaging his hand. "*Gah!* This is so much easier when I have some protection for my hands!"

Jess used the bonuses granted to her by her new armor to dodge and weave through the expanding troop of monkeys, taking light damage but unable to deal any herself. "Jaxon! Drop and roll left!"

Jaxon dropped as soon as he heard her but rolled to the right before her words were complete. He got stepped on but was able to avoid the surefire critical that would have torn open his back. He had the wind knocked out of him, and it took a hard *shift* to open his airway. Eight monkeys had charged into battle with them, and without weapons, the humans were starting to have a tough time holding them off. Jaxon started to land crippling or disabling blows, intent on making it difficult to be overrun by sheer numbers.

In a few moments, his efforts started to bear fruit, and the primates began to slow. Whether it was because the creatures were attacking slower thanks to twisted limbs or simply moving on legs with severe and sudden cramps, the tide began to turn against them. Jaxon knocked one over and sharply punched it in the jaw four times before rolling backward and activating Adjust. The mandible he had targeted shifted and broke, causing serious pain and disorientation. While the beast flailed on the ground, Jaxon landed a heavy blow to its neck, cutting off air and blood flow.

"Jaw-dropping action! One down, seven to go." Jaxon bent his knees, bobbed in place, then splayed his hands and wiggled them tauntingly at the remaining troop. His non-official skills in inciting violence were near mythical by themselves, which was proven as the remaining opponents rushed at him while howling furiously. Jaxon twisted to the left as the first strike came down, jumped over an attempted tackle, and weaved between a pincer tactic. He took every available opportunity to lash out with an attack of his own, landing a few critical hits over the course of a few seconds.

This wasn't enough to take any of the beasts down, and they began to rotate away from him if they took too heavy of a blow. He couldn't pursue them without opening himself up to all sorts of attacks of opportunity, and they seemed to know it. "*Jump!*"

Jaxon heard Jess speak and took to the air as soon as her words registered. Two primates crossed in the air under him, having attempted to bring him to the ground with flying tackles from either side. As Jaxon was coming back to the ground, he felt something click in his mind and realized that his newest skill had just finished cooling down. He settled on the ground and found himself in a swiftly closing ring of bodies.

"I'm surrounded!" Jaxon exclaimed with false horror before allowing his true feelings to shine through. "Attacking in any direction it is! *Living Weapons!*"

"*Craw?*"

"*Nyah!*"

Jaxon's hands blurred and were replaced by T-Rex heads. They made some interesting sounds, perhaps inquisitive or interested vocalizations. The primates, either not realizing the danger or disregarding it, continued their attack. Jaxon lashed out with his arm the same way he would with a straight punch, not having any control of his hands other than to direct them. The jaws of his hand opened and tore into the monkey's face, and as Jaxon pulled back his hand, a good chunk of its cheek came with it.

Another fist flew out, and Lefty latched onto one of the beast's clavicle. Jaxon tried to pull his hand back, but the feral T-Rex head refused to let go of its prey. Clawed paws tore long strips of Jaxon's sides open, and he growled in fury.

Intimidation success!

Lefty let go of the monkey and turned toward Jaxon with a low **hiss**. Jaxon glared back at it, even while swinging Terror into range of an unprotected throat. The long, sharp, sturdy teeth tore through the soft flesh with ease. The monkey dropped to the ground with a wet gurgle, and Terror swallowed the chunk of meat it had taken.

Mana restored: 38.

"Behind you, Jaxon!" Jess hadn't been idle, taking any opportunity to distract or attack the creatures who were focused heavily on the Monk.

"What! If they eat during combat they last longer?" Jaxon turned and drove Lefty into the stomach of the primate charging from behind. He crouched and pushed, lifting and throwing the creature over himself while his left head-hand tore through its entrails.

Mana restored: 54.

"That's a full second's worth of mana!" Jaxon laughed as gore rained down on him, looking like a psychotic murderer for all purposes. He pushed up and off the ground, jumping and using his superior weight to take one of the monkeys to the grass. Instead of punching repeatedly, he simply pressed his hands into the monkey and let his hands grab mouthfuls of fresh meat. Then he *yanked* back, allowing them to tear the meat off and swallow it.

Jaxon was having too much fun to realize how many blows he was taking, but the damage was beginning to add up. A paw slapped against the back of his head, tearing furrows in the skin and nearly cracking his skull. If his bones hadn't been more flexible than normal, that might have even given him a serious injury. He rolled forward over the now-still monkey and sprang back into battle. His hands gripped onto a pair of furry shoulders, the teeth digging deeply into the animal's body. Through the adrenaline, Jaxon noticed that the T-Rex heads had found a good spot, and he wanted to try his other abilities in tandem with the Living Weapons. "*Adjust.*"

Wherever the teeth were grazing a joint, there was a sickening *pop*. A wall of damage notifications appeared in front of Jaxon, and his prey shuddered and stilled. He made sure to tear out a small feast for his hands as he turned to engage the others and was able to finish off the few undamaged creatures in only a few seconds. Holding down the final monkey, Jaxon moved his hands like pistons, allowing them to eat their fill.

When they seemed to want no more, he turned them toward himself and smiled at them. "We are going to have you sample the flesh of thousands of beasts! We will restore the T-Rex as the apex predator in this world! Ah... at least T-Rex *heads*!"

"Craw!"

"Nyah!

After a few seconds of inactivity, his hands returned to being *just* hands, and Jaxon sighed contentedly. There was a wall of blinking notifications waiting for him, so he started with the most recent, filtering out the combat damage logs.

Experience gained: 200 (25 * Trial Primate x8).

As this is the first time you have made a kill with your Living Weapons, new information has been unlocked! You can choose to devote the experience from the kills to either leveling up Living Weapons, devote it to your specialization to increase your class level, or allow the experience to flow to your character level. These options can be changed at any time but must be done before combat. Where would you like the experience to go for now?

"To the weapons," Jaxon responded to the prompt as soon as he finished reading the text.

Experience division set!

Your Living Weapons' disposition has shifted from 'Feral' to 'Wild'. They are now 10% less likely to attack you if they come in range! Levels of disposition are: Feral, Wild, Confused, Timid, Placid, Poorly Trained, Trained, Obedient, Fully Tamed. There are many ways to move through dispositions; try to find what works best for your creatures!

Skill increase: Adjust (Expert VI)

Skill increase: Body Compression (Novice III)

Skill increase: Contortionist's Dodge (Student 0)

Congratulations! You have regained the Student Rank for a skill you sacrificed! Title gained: Power's Cost.

Skill increase: Jump (Apprentice I)

Skill increase: Living Weapon (Novice II)

Title gained: Power's Cost: You have given up skill levels, not to combine them but to gain something greater. Now,

*through dedicated effort, you have regained the lost ranking! +1
to each stat except Karmic Luck!*

*Assassin Class unlocked! Would you like to replace your
current class with 'Assassin'? Yes / No.*

"No." There was only one remaining, so Jaxon finally
looked at the notification that had been blinking at him since he
first got his T-Rex Head Hands.

*Quest complete: Finding a specialization! You have
listened to your heart and followed the true path of a Monk.
Optional requirement of gaining a class and specializing without
joining a party* technically *completed: Reward: New skill.*

*Passive skill gained: Battle Meditation (Novice I). You
are not designed to sit still to clear your mind. Your mind is
focused and true to itself only when* doing *things. Effect: Skills
costing Mana or Stamina cost .5n% less after you have been in
combat for at least five seconds, where 'n' equals skill level.*

CHAPTER TWENTY-THREE

Jess and Jaxon were making good time through the forest. Now that they knew the general direction they should be going, they were able to move over the terrain much faster. The two of them had made an official party now that Jaxon's quest had been completed and had been working to test their new capabilities. Jess had armed herself once more with sharp claws taken from the rampaging primates and was at least able to deal *some* damage in the recent battles.

While they were sitting to recover from a small fight, Jaxon started looking over his skills and stat sheet. His new class seemed to be intentionally difficult to understand, so he was trying to figure out how everything interacted. He hadn't been able to re-summon his Living Weapons, but the only change he noticed when the skill went up in rank was a small reduction to its cooldown, a *very* small reduction. The thirty-minute cooldown had turned into a twenty-nine point seven-nine cooldown. That was only a... *point* two-five-five reduction per level!

The Mana cost had moved from fifty a second to forty-five per second, but he wasn't sure if that was due to the skill level or the disposition aspect of things. He pulled open his character sheet and took a look at his current stats.

Name: Jaxon 'Legend' Class: **Bonecruncher**
Profession: Chiropractor
Bonecruncher Level: 1 Exp: 0 Exp to next level: 1,000
Level: 12 Exp: 78,026 Exp to next level: 12,774

Hit Points: 425/440 (50+(380)) (Base 50 plus 10 points for each point in Constitution, once it has increased above 10.)

Mana: 337.5/337.5 (12.5*27) (12.5 mana per point of Intelligence.)

Mana regen: 9 (.25*27) (Wisdom multiplied by .25 mana regen per second)

Stamina: 415/565 (50+(315)+(190)) (Base 50 plus 5 points for each point in strength and constitution, once each of the stats has increased above 10.)

Characteristic: Raw score (Modifier)

Strength: 74 (2.24)
Dexterity: 101 (3.01)
Constitution: 49 (1.49)
Intelligence: 27 (1.27)
Wisdom: 36 (1.36)
Charisma: 6 (0.06)
Perception: 22 (1.22)
Luck: 46 (1.46)
Karmic Luck: +2

Not a huge amount had changed, but when the page came up, he noticed that a new tab had been added. He opened it and was given a stat sheet for his living weapons!

Name: Lefty and Terror Class: Living Weapons
Level: 1 Exp: 175 Exp to next level: 825

Characteristic: Raw score (Modifier)

Strength: 37 (1.37)
Dexterity: 50 (2.0)
Intelligence: 13 (1.13)
Wisdom: 18 (1.18)
Perception: 33 (1.33)

The stat sheet was simpler than his own, which made sense. The weapons didn't have their own health pool; they were *his* hands. They also didn't have mana or stamina of their own, using Jaxon's to operate. There was a small section under the stats that vanished after he read it, but luckily, it had been easy to understand.

Statistics are calculated as: User's stats divided by two, plus one point per two levels for every stat except Perception, which gains three points per two levels. Living Weapon's level cannot exceed user's own character level.

Jaxon looked at his own stats then the weapon's and dropped his head between his knees. His *hands* had better perception than he did—by a full ten points. Jess shook his arm, beckoning for him to rise. "We need to keep moving, Jaxon. Night is going to fall in a few hours, and I have no interest in getting out of this forest the wrong way."

"I was just looking over the stats for my new skills, didn't mean to go off into my own world there!" Jaxon popped to his feet, and they began trudging toward their goal, the Wolfman outpost. They only had a solid day of travel left, having worked out a more direct path than the one they had arrived on.

Night has arrived in the forest of trials. Doubling the number of predatory monsters in the zone. Good luck on your survival!

"Do you think we took too long of a break there?" Jess questioned as they hurried along their chosen path, slowed only by the need to go around any trees in their way.

"If we somehow *did* take too long of a rest, would it help us in any way to ruminate on it?" Jaxon tossed a response at her, and she went silent for a few minutes as she thought about it. The silence stretched long enough that Jaxon was actually starting to feel comfortable around her.

Then she started to speak, "I guess not? Maybe that is my real issue in life. I always think on the things that I *did* instead of the things I want to or should do."

Jess paused and licked her lips. "I guess wisdom comes with age, huh?"

"That's not wisdom. That's common sense, or at least, it was. The past is the past, the present is gone, and the future is all we have." Jaxon grinned about his revised sayings. "You think that your past is what has been holding you back? Or... would you *like* it to be what is holding you back so that you have an excuse not to *try?*"

"*Excuse* me?" Jess raised her brows and dared Jaxon to continue speaking.

"Done!" Jaxon nodded at her words. "All is forgiven, then. From what I have seen, you have some talent as a tactician. It's unrefined, and I think you freeze up mid-combat. Either that or you are *really* quiet. You have admitted that this is what interests you. What is stopping you from applying to one of the big guilds and getting training and experience?"

"Nothing, *now!*" Jess quipped, hoping that playing this off would make Jaxon go silent so she could focus on running. "*You're* bringing me on!"

"Yes, yes, but before that you were planning to settle into a guild you didn't like, doing things you didn't like, with people that are pretty unlikeable." Jaxon had a concerned look on his face when she dared to look over. "Again, you have a *talent* that many people don't have, but you seem like you'd rather not even try. What can I do to help you? Here or in real life, there will always be someone willing to take a stand for you, even if you don't believe it."

Jess shook her head. "Jaxon, I lost a dagger that is currently unique to the guild of player killers. I might be safe from them in the middle of a huge guild, but there are going to be times when I am alone or my group is small enough to be taken down. Unless I figure out a way to replace the dagger, I'm going to be blacklisted for a long time, and they have plenty of money for setting up bounties, legal or not."

"Fine, I'll buy out your debt. What will it take?" Jaxon rolled his eyes when she shook her head.

"It's not that easy. They won't accept money, not for this." Jess glared at Jaxon. "I'm serious! The dagger is an item that lets you loot a *player* when you kill them with it, and it can only be gained in a really dangerous area that the guild either owns or is the only group to know it's location. Going through that area and getting your own dagger is the only way to join the guild, and I lost the one that had been loaned to me for my mission. Now I would need to go through it and give up my reward weapon *just* to get off their blacklist. They'd still hate me, though."

"I'll ask the Wolfmen for the dagger when we get back. Alternatively, what if we *both* went through and gave up the dagger? Then they are getting out more than they put in and would have no reasonable complaint against you." Jaxon smiled at her shocked expression; it was a nice shift.

"I couldn't ask you to do that. I told you, the area is *super* dangerous. Also, apparently, if you don't make it through there, you can never attempt it again." Jess's eyes were on the darkening forest ahead of her as she spoke. "You can only go back if you clear the place every time you go through it. If we screwed it up..."

"Good thing we are getting all this practice working together, huh?" Jaxon's eyes were bright, and his maniacal smile even made Jess's lips twitch. "I'll go if you will let me, and then you'll have no excuses for working to become a powerhouse in my guild. Deal?"

"I guess it's a deal." Jess waited for a notification, a quest or something to pop up at her. Jaxon had just seemed so *Noble* and sincere, so it was a little disappointing that she only had his word and not a system assurance. She shook that thought off; at least he was trying.

Ah-whooo! The hunting call of the Trial Primates sounded near them, confirming that they had been found and another fight was on the way.

As the first of the Primates broke stealth to attack Jaxon, he laughed and retaliated. He activated Living Weapons and struck back with a T-Rex head hand, "Guess what came off cooldown? Looks like meat is on the menu, boys! Eat up!"

"*Craw!*"

"*Nyah!*"

CHAPTER TWENTY-FOUR

Jaxon and Jess stumbled into the Wolfman outpost a little over a day later, getting under a lean-to that was used to dry wood and falling into a deep sleep. They woke up to the sound of chuffing laughter, Wolfmen Warriors surrounding them and laughing at their sorry state.

Jaxon popped up and got close to one of them, his mud-and-dirt coated face being split by dazzlingly white teeth. He slipped into speaking their language, poorly, "Rawrdrick! You've been working on your straight-stand! I am is pleased!"

"My name is pronounced Rod-rick, feisty man flesh." Rodrick chuffed as Jaxon visibly tried to translate what was being said.

"Is there way we track down who took her metal sharp-stick?" Jaxon pointed at Jess who was watching the conversation with a wary expression.

"No chance. I know who has it. He left for the war-front two days ago."

The human shrugged and moved on. "You is doing move positions I told you? Bad standing come back if not worked at!"

"Yes, I am doing the exercises you prescribed." Rodrick sighed as the others in his group chuffed at his discomfort. "What are you doing here? Are you going to be setting up your shop again?"

"Oh!" Jaxon thought for a moment. "Am doing, yes. Stay in camp short while, train hands by trial. Then is going leave, fight hairless annoyances!"

"Training your hands? I have no idea what you are saying." Rodrick turned to the others and spoke fast enough that

Jaxon didn't have a chance to follow along, "Heh. I convinced him that 'hairless annoyance' is our word for Humans."

The Wolfmen dispersed, laughing at that, but Jaxon stopped Rodrick from leaving and looked at him with a serious face. He switched to English and asked a question, "Rawrdrick, we need to improve quickly, and the Trial Primates are good experience for us right now. Is there any way I can get quests for them and do something for you at the same time?"

Rodrick tilted his head to the side and flicked his ears before responding in broken English, "I... hmmm. You bring meat, bring fur, I convince for rewards."

"You're a good boy." Jaxon punched Rodrick gently, then adjusted that spot with a thought. A minor posture issue was fixed, and the Wolfman decided not to take offense at the familiarity.

"What's happening, Jaxon?" Jess stood up and scratched at the dried blood on her neck. "How did you learn their language, by the way?"

"It was a quest reward," Jaxon responded faintly, trying to plan their next move. "We need weapons and armor. I think I can trade a few adjustments for some basic weapons, but metal is a really big deal to these guys. They won't give that kind of thing up cheaply if at all. Then I want to go back into the trial area and work on training Lefty and Terror to an acceptable level. We can gather pelts and meat, trading them for quest rewards, experience, and reputation. Sound like a plan?"

"Works for me, Jaxon. Shall we get to it then?" Jess had planned to go bathe or find *some* way to get clean, but she knew wandering too far from Jaxon's side would inevitably result in her getting eaten.

They went into the same location Jaxon had previously offered buffs, and he was soon gaining small amounts of trade goods. It seemed that a large amount of the Warriors in the area had left and gone to join in the common defense of their shattered and leaderless race. For some reason, there didn't seem to be much concern from the Wolfmen in this area. Any time the topic was brought up, they gave their version of a shrug and moved on.

Jaxon took the pile of smoked meats and various baubles over to a weapons merchant and traded every single bit of it for a matching pair of stone-reinforced bone daggers. He handed them over to Jess with a smile and then got back to work, this time saving up for a meal and a bath. This was easier, especially since most of the goods given to them were food based, but after eventually conveying their desire to the Wolfmen, they found that baths were not a thing in this culture.

"Sorry, Jess, looks like we're gonna have to go without being clean for a while. I hope you don't mind. I know I don't." Jaxon shrugged at her horrified expression and decided to move on. "I did get an interesting offer from a tanner and a leatherworker, though. I'll get one cured hide per five raw pelts that I bring in, and the leatherworker will make me boots and a pair of studded gloves if I give him five cured hides. He said something about learning a new design or something."

"They are robbing you blind, Jaxon." Jess shook her head at his cheerful acceptance of the trade values.

"Good thing I won't be able to *see* it then, huh?" He waggled his bushy eyebrows at her, and she shuddered as her only reply. "It's fine; we need to go out there and fight the Primates for experience anyway. I got another thousand on the way out yesterday, but my T-Rex Head Hands only got six hundred the whole day."

"Do you think we should go out and hunt at night? That way we can maximize the number of creatures that we fight, and you'll be able to keep your hands out longer. That is, keep them transformed. What the heck, that's so weird to say out loud." Jess grimaced and looked away in disgust, making Jaxon laugh.

"How about later in the day and into the night? I'm not a huge fan of messing up my sleep schedule just to do a little hunting." Jaxon made a good point, and they decided to go back to sleep, filth and all. The little lean-to didn't offer much in the way of protection from the elements, mainly being a way to stay out of sight and mind. Luckily, they were tired enough that they slept the majority of the day, only waking up after most of the Wolfmen were finishing their dinner. Jess and Jaxon sat wearily in their little shelter and ate some pungent, smoked jerky, comparing their debuffs.

"I have stinky level three and poorly rested," Jess complained bitterly, really feeling the hit to her charisma.

"*When I walk around my neighborhood, I feed dogs meat with broken glass in it to stop their incessant barking.*" Jaxon's words made Jess recoil as if she had been slapped, but she paused before snapping at him and cocked her head to the side.

"Jaxon, what did you just say?"

"I *said*: stinky level four, mental fatigue two, and *seepage three.*" Jaxon shook his head sadly. "*There are many ways to skin a cat, but I think I found the* best *way.*"

"Right, okay, Jaxon, don't answer out loud, but do your debuffs to charisma put you at *negative* charisma right now?" Jess's words seemed to reach him, and Jaxon looked off into space for a moment before nodding. "Alright. Do me a favor? Do your best not to talk until after we find a way to clear up the debuffs to your charisma? You are slightly more evil and terrifying than usual right now."

Jaxon cackled wickedly, agreeing by smiling and nodding at her while leering. Jess felt the bile rise in her throat as he squirmed to his feet and started stalking toward the trial area. "Hurry up, Jess. There are *creatures to murder for fresh meat*."

"What did I *just* tell you?" Jess muttered as she hurried to keep up with him. He was skipping away, but instead of the normal strange look he had while doing this, Jaxon was posed like a velociraptor. He completed this look by screeching intermittently, and Jess would have found it funny if she at all believed that he was doing it intentionally.

Jaxon's only reply to her question was a screech like someone sucking in air to sound like a dinosaur. He got to the rear wall of the outpost and *jumped*, somehow clearing the eight-foot wall with ease. Unfortunately, this left Jess in a Wolfman outpost without a neutral party to vouch for her. She scrambled to get over the wall, managing to escape just as the first spear stuck into it where her lower back had been a moment prior. She was shaken and sprinted after the skipping Monk with a dark look on her face.

Jaxon's high-pitched sounds were already drawing Primates to him, which was an unexpected benefit to his currently debuffed state. He took two hits before he was able to see the monkeys, since Jess had been too far away to call out a warning in time. She caught up to him just as he grabbed the creature by the neck and chucked it at a nearby tree. With a crack and a *splat*, the beast was crushed by a wooden force of nature. Jaxon howled in triumph even as the creatures surrounding him became enraged.

Jess shouted a few detailed instructions and joined the fight, driving her new daggers into the kidney area of a monkey that was looking toward Jaxon. The pain made the beast go rigid, and she kicked it in the back of the knees to force it to the ground. She reached around the creature as if she were giving it a hug, then tore open its neck with both daggers. She started to get swept up in the battle and shouted into the air with her blood-soaked daggers held to either side, "I'm *back*, baby!"

Shouting was a bad decision, as Jess had caught the attention of the monkeys. Seeing their comrade brought down made them hop up and down, howling for reinforcements. The crashing in the undergrowth around the humans let them know that the battle was about to heat up... but this was exactly what Jaxon wanted. He pulled back his fist to throw a punch, activating Living Weapons as his hand started to move forward. His simple punch turned into a serrated grip, and by twisting his hand as he moved backward and triggering Adjust, his target's shoulder was dislocated as well as shredded.

The Primate turned and ran, but by the amount of blood pouring out of its wound, escaping for now wouldn't matter. Jaxon turned his weapons on the other creatures coming, and— thanks to Jess finally being useful in combat—soon the remainder of foes had either been defeated or had fled. Out of enemies, Jaxon turned toward Jess to ask a question. He forgot that his hands were wild, and Terror got close enough to latch onto the bicep of his left arm. Jaxon shouted in pain but was somehow able to manage not to instinctively yank his arm away, as that would have only created more damage.

He glared down at Terror, who was starting to chew. Jaxon shouted again, this time in rage. He leaned down and *chomped* onto the back of Terror, dumping the entirety of his stamina into his intimidation skill as he did so. "*Ragh!*"

Terror instinctively released Jaxon's bicep and seemed to recoil in shock. Jaxon's health began depleting rapidly, not only from blood loss and the damage to his arm but he was biting and chewing on his own hand as hard as he could. He managed to break through the leathery skin and draw blood, then pulled back with his arm and let go. Glowering at the T-Rex head, he shouted, "*No! Bad* Terror!"

His hands stared at him for an additional two seconds, and neither of the parties involved moved until his hands reverted into *just* hands.

Your Living Weapons' disposition has shifted from 'Wild' to 'Confused'. They are now 20% less likely to attack you if they come in range!

Jaxon quickly pulled up his skill and looked at it before reading any of the other notifications. Just as he suspected, the mana cost to maintain his Living Weapons had decreased again and was now sitting at forty mana per second. "Excellent. When they are fully tamed, they should cost... only ten mana per second? Wonderful!"

Experience gained: 25 (25 * Trial Primate x1)

Experience gained (Living Weapon): 225 (25 * Trial Primate x9)

Your Living Weapons have reached level 2!

Skill increased: Living Weapons (Novice V).

"Did you *bite* yourself?" Jess asked Jaxon as she moved forward and wrapped a cloth tightly around his bicep. "I don't know if I can handle being around you, man."

"Ah, don't worry about it." Jaxon sighed as he sat down. In fact, he very nearly passed out since his Mana and stamina were both almost at zero. "It's an old dog training trick. If a dog bites you, you either have to pry open its mouth by pressing on the hinges of its jaw or you need to bite it on the ear. Terror didn't have an ear, so I just bit down."

Jess didn't respond, so Jaxon tried to think of what he could do now that combat had ended. His eyes lit up as he remembered that he had a slew of skill points to assign, and he pulled open his skill sheet to do just that. Ten skill points... what to do with them...

CHAPTER TWENTY-FIVE

As the sun rose over the Wolfman outpost, Jess and Jaxon stumbled back into town with a heavy load of bloody pelts and raw meat being dragged behind them. Jaxon smiled up at the Wolfmen on the wall who were looking down with amusement, letting go of his burden to wave. "Give you both meat, five chunk, you help lift?"

His terrible accent and word pronunciation made the Wolfmen wince, but they agreed and helped bring in the sticky mass of loot. Jaxon was pleased with the choices he had made over the course of the night. Firstly, he had only assigned five of his available points. This had brought his Acupressure skill back up to the Master Rank and had given him a secondary benefit in the form of a notification.

Title upgraded: Power's Cost II. You have given up skill levels, not to combine them but to gain something greater. Now, through dedicated effort, you have regained the lost Master ranking! +2 to each stat except Karmic Luck! (Does not stack with Power's Cost rank I).

This had caused his constitution stat to hit the benchmark of fifty points, and he had fallen to the ground writhing in pain until his body had become denser and far heartier. Luckily for him, this transition had mostly closed the open wounds on his arm formed by his T-Rex hand, but since he hadn't given Jess any warning, she thought that he was poisoned or some other effect. She had a minor panic attack before realizing what was going on.

Over the course of the night, they had continuously hunted the Primates. Their plans to come back to town halfway through the night had been thwarted by the sheer number of opponents, but they had become somewhat accustomed to the sleep deprivation and had powered through... to great effect. Jaxon looked at the accumulated notifications as they walked toward the tanner in the town.

Skill increased: Aerial acrobatics (Beginner VII).

Skill increased: Battle Meditation (Novice IX).

Skill increased: Body Compression (Novice V).

Skill increased: Cloth Armor Mastery (Beginner IX).

Skill increased: Contortionist's Dodge (Apprentice III).

Skill increased: Intimidation (Journeyman VII).

Skill increased: Jump (Apprentice V).

Skill increased: Living Weapons (Novice IX).

Experience gained: 400 (25 * Trial Primate x16)

Experience gained (Living Weapon): 2,000 (25 * Trial Primate x80)

Your Living Weapons have reached level 3!

It had been a great night in terms of increasing skills, and he had found that Battle Meditation had been used near constantly. Also, once he had regained his Master rank in Acupressure, he was nearly salivating over the information he once again had access to. He had a nearly *overwhelming* desire to bring Adjust back into the Master ranks, but something kept holding him back from making the commitment.

Thanks to generous usage over the night, he had also come to understand his living weapons to a higher degree. Jaxon hadn't been certain what it would mean for them to have their own stat sheet, but it seemed that it created an additive effect with his own abilities. So, if his T-Rex heads were at thirty points of strength and Jaxon was at fifty, he could let them attack on their own, *or* he could put his own strength behind blows. This would turn that 'thirty' and 'fifty' into *eighty* points of strength being behind an attack.

Of course, it wasn't a *perfect* conversion, but the damage he saw was *about* what he would expect to see at that level. In terms of growth, the passive skill had easily increased the most over the night, which was nice, but Jaxon was most excited over his T-Rex Head Hands almost getting to the next tier. Something fun would happen; he was sure of it. Jaxon wanted to just *make* it happen but once more decided against spending the points.

"These... useless," the Tanner was complaining about some of the pelts they had turned in, specifically the ones that had been savaged by the Living Weapons. "I won't take them."

"I'm *certain* that you didn't mention that a pelt had to be at a specific quality." Jaxon's eyes glittered savagely, though he held his smile in place. "I'm sure you wouldn't go back on a quest reward now, right?"

Contrary to expectations, the Wolfman only chuffed in reply. "Who offered a quest? I told you what my rates were for work. You have enough here of a good enough quality... I'll give you six cured pelts for all of this or four for only the non-trash quality ones."

"Done!" Jaxon cheerfully replied. The Tanner nodded and retrieved six pelts, handing them over with his ears forward and twitching, both of which were obvious signs of excitement and happiness.

"Are you kidding me?" Jess hissed at him. "We made three trips to get all these hides into the outpost! There are almost *ninety* of them, and you are trading them for *six*?"

"What?" Jaxon glanced at her with a confused expression. "I only *needed* five!"

She scoffed as they walked to the Leatherworker, who took Jaxon's measurements and told him to come back in a few hours. Jaxon gifted him the additional hide as a tip to get the best quality work. Then they went over to the communal dining area of the Wolfmen and made sure that all of the meat had made its way into the building.

Reputation increase: You have given the Wolfmen enough food to last their entire outpost a week if properly rationed. In this time of war, where their fighters are away, this will help the outpost thrive! +1200 reputation. Current reputation with Wolfmen: 0 (forced neutral). Actual reputation: -1000 (Cautious).

"Pain-power man!" a pup called over to Jaxon in its high-pitched voice. "You smell like poop-pit! Go to river, rising sun side of town!"

"Thank you, puppy!" Jaxon called back in English, getting only a cocked head in response. The pup didn't know any words except its own people's. "Look at that, Jess! I got enough reputation that people will tell me that I stink and where to find a river!"

"If I knew where it was, I would have taken you there myself a *long* time ago," Jess muttered. "Whatever, at least we have something to do except sleep while we wait for your boots and gloves that couldn't *possibly* take more than two hides to make.

They left the outpost and went to the river, disrobing and getting into the water when they found a spot that allowed for a bit of privacy for both of them. After they were clean, they started doing their best to wash their clothes; then they waited in the water for the clothes to dry.

Hiss... Jaxon looked over to see a snake rearing its head out of the water and swimming closer to him. He slowly started waving his arms and doing his best to distract the creature. It slowed, then began following the movements of his arms and undulating body. "Jess? Hey, Jess!"

"What?" the reply came from behind a curtain of hanging vines and leaves.

"I'm charming a snake over here. Want to come over and take a look?" Jaxon called carefully.

"Why are men so disgusting? I *don't* want to hear about it, Jaxon!" Jess's tone was scathing. "I have no interest in your 'one-eyed snake'!"

Jaxon took a closer look at the serpent in the water. Indeed, it seemed that this snake had been in a fight that had caused its eye to be replaced with scar tissue. "Oh-ho-ho! Spying on my side, are you? I didn't even see that until you pointed it out, naughty girl! Oh, careful! It's floating toward you!"

The snake, now calm, was allowing the river currents to drag it downstream. Jess didn't seem to understand what he was saying until a minute later when a scream reached Jaxon's ears, "*Snake!*"

"Yeah, I told you about that basically *forever* ago!" Jaxon called back to her.

"I thought you were being disgusting!"

"Nope, there was a snake."

"I can *see* that, Jaxon!" Jess got out of the water at that point and put on her still-damp clothes. "I don't know what you did to it, but it totally ignored me, at least."

"I already *told* you! I charmed it!" Jaxon laughed at the low sigh that traveled over the water. "I'm getting out now. Avert your eyes. I'm shy or something."

They walked back into the outpost a few minutes later, deciding to get the new gear before going to sleep. They had to waste some time and so ate some food and rested a little, but soon enough, Jaxon was wearing an odd set of gloves and boots that fit *very* comfortably. The gloves went on his hands, then had extremely long strips of leather that wrapped around his arms almost all the way to his shoulder. The Leatherworker explained that gloves like this were used to help train their pups and had guessed that Jaxon needed something like this since he had bite scars all over his arms.

After they had finished taking a nap and relieving their fatigue, it was finally time to leave the outpost behind and finish their personal journey. Jaxon looked over at Jess and cracked his knuckles. "Are you ready to go and force a guild to leave you alone?"

"So ready," Jess affirmed with a tight smile.

"Excellent." Jaxon helped her over the wall, and they started walking away from the outpost. "So. Where are we going?"

"Not a clue."

"Wait, what?"

"I only know where they go drinking and recruit people. I have no idea where they go to get the daggers." Jess didn't look directly at Jaxon as she spoke. "The rest I only know as rumors."

"So... we're going to go to a bar then?" Jaxon nodded at this thought; he could use a drink after this whole debacle. "How far away is this place?"

"Probably two days if we go really slowly, also accounting for the time that we will likely need in order to fight off creatures and the like." Jess sped up a bit, trying to set a better pace.

"Look at that! Already planning out our route and setting us up for success!" Jaxon smiled happily as he matched her speed. "We'll make a tactician out of you yet!"

CHAPTER TWENTY-SIX

They made it into the small town with a few hours to spare. Jess's prediction had been accurate, but Jaxon had been able to cut down on monster attacks by learning a new method of using intimidation. By intentionally and slowly allowing stamina to pour into the skill, it had created an aura effect that drove creatures away. Jaxon was almost *certain* that this would turn into a skill if he continued to use it in this manner and was put off when no skill appeared before him.

Not wanting to charge into a possible battle while poorly-rested and hungry, they went into the inn of the town and arranged for a bed and bath. Unsurprisingly, the bar was attached to the inn, but luckily, the owner had seen fit to have them somewhat separated. Perhaps they simply had loud drunks in this town? Either way, the two slept through the night after getting clean and went down to the bar for breakfast.

The room was mostly empty but for a few day-drinkers nursing hangovers. The two each ordered a plate of fried eggs and slices of ham and were nearly finished when a smirking man sauntered over. "*Jess*, how very *surprising* that you would show up here! I've been looking for a way to get some brownie points with our fearless leader, and poof, you show up! Don't take this too personally. It's just business."

With no additional warning, a dagger slithered into his palm and he lashed out, attempting to stab her in the eye. Jaxon's fist slammed into his wrist and forced the blade into the wood of the seat, but the man didn't seem bothered. "Oh? Hello there. Got anything good I can take?"

"Literally wearing everything I brought with me," Jaxon responded brightly.

"Money?"

"Not a copper to my name." Jaxon picked up a chunk of ham and chewed away at it.

"Oh? And how were you planning to pay for your breakfast?" the Rogue asked in a strangely polite tone. "Or the room you rented last night?"

The secret ingredient..." Jaxon swallowed, locked eyes with the man, and whispered, "is *crime.*"

"Ha!" The man took a step back and grinned at them. "Alright, you've got my attention. Why are you here, and why would it be better to take you to the guild instead of killing you both?"

"We're here to get your guild a couple of daggers, and you should take us with you because I think the guy who ran out of here when you stabbed the chair went to get the guards." Jaxon stood up, pushing his chair back as he did so. "Also because in an enclosed area like this, you can't defeat me alone. No chance."

"Oh, for..." Jess facepalmed and looked at Jaxon with a pained expression. "There's five of them around us, Jaxon. A guild of assassins and player killers, remember?"

"Well, that makes more sense." Jaxon nodded gravely. "Still, we are planning to get you the daggers and just hand them over. Sounds nice, right?"

"I don't think you know what you're getting into, but sure." The smiling man motioned for them to follow along. "Come on; you can chat with the boss."

Jaxon and Jess started walking to the door, but Mr. Smiles didn't move, simply watching them as they took a few steps and collapsed to the ground, unconscious. "Pah. Really, coming into our town, our bar, and eating the food? Morons. Alrighty boy-o's! Load 'em up. Move 'em out!"

Status effect: Unconscious. Time remaining: 3... 2... 1...

Jaxon snapped back to awareness instantly, curiously not needing to step through the portal from his respawn room. His hands were tied behind his back, connected by rope to the chair as well as his feet. Jess snapped awake next to him, finding herself in the same position. She sighed and shrugged. "Well, that's a good lesson, I guess."

"Life lessons are *so* important these days." A man faded into existence in front of them, somehow remaining translucent and hard to keep track of. "Why did you lose my dagger, Jess?"

"Got captured by a squad of Wolfmen." Jess sighed as the man rolled his eyes. "Look, BackAttack, not everyone can kill thirty of the beasts when they are standing next to each other without them noticing. We're here to make up for it. We want to earn our own daggers, then we will turn *both* of them over to you. Will that clear my record?"

"You don't know what you're asking to do. We are a guild of glorified muggers, trying to eventually become this world's best Assassin guild, but even I'm not that heartless. The game can do things to you in the dungeon that we can't, and wouldn't." BackAttack sat down on a much more comfortable-looking chair. "How about you just let us kill you off every time we find you for... oh, six months?"

"*Six months?*" Jess looked like she was about to gag.

"What's the deal?" Jaxon interjected. "Why can't I just give you a sack of gold and we can forget about this whole thing?"

BackAttack shook his head. "Don't need it. I was one of the top three contributors to the Wolfman war. I have plenty of cash. Nope, what I need is a way for my guild to expand and become more than it is. Lots of people out there wanting to do what we do, and we need an advantage. The daggers are the thing. Look at these."

He held up two matching daggers, which looked familiar to Jess and yet... subtly different. "This is the upgraded form of our weapon. After we kill two hundred and fifty different people with a dagger, we can go through the dungeon again and exchange it for this upgraded version. Double the damage and... well... I suppose you don't need to know our secrets, hmm?"

"Lets you get experience for killing people, huh?" Jaxon stated aloud, causing the first emotion beyond annoyance to appear on BackAttack's face.

"Who told you that? Can you inspect weapons from a distance?" The man snarled in Jaxon's face, a dagger held to his jugular.

"I just guessed. I figured it was a natural evolution to a dagger that lets you steal items from people." Jaxon tried to shrug but ended up cutting himself on the dagger. "Ow."

"You know too much." BackAttack slid back, rubbing his hand through his hair. "You know what? Whatever. You want to try to get one of these, go for it. I'm warning you now, though, you'll probably die. This is an area designed for the sneaky and the perceptive."

"Here is what I propose: we'll give you a dagger if you promise to stop hunting Jess," Jaxon stated defiantly before pausing for a second. "Also, if you leave me alone as well. No hunting me either."

"Sure, so long as you agree not to tell others about the daggers, and *if* you survive getting a dagger." BackAttack shook his head and stood, planning to let them out of the chairs.

"Deal. Shake on it?" Jaxon thrust a hand forward, once more surprising BackAttack.

"How did you get free?" He suspiciously looked at the hand for signs of thread or cut rope.

"I bend really easily." Jaxon smiled widely and continued to hold his hand in the air. "Do we have an agreement?"

"Sure." They shook, and a notification appeared in front of them.

Deal struck! Both parties will be notified if the other party fails to uphold their side of the agreement. The first to break the agreement will gain a Warlock title.

"By the way, I'm not sure if you know this, but I'm part of The Wanderer's guild. If you break this deal, I will do everything I can to burn your guild to the ground," Jaxon stated this as cheerfully as if he had been talking to a friend while eating bacon.

BackAttack stiffened, but an ugly smile appeared on his face. "Lovely. You know what? I think that this might work out after all. Can I offer you a drink?"

"The knockout stuff again?"

"Yup."

"Fine..." Jaxon sighed, understanding that they wouldn't survive leaving this place any other way. Jaxon and Jess both drank a surprisingly tasty smoothie, and the last thing Jaxon said was, "Stupid Assassins and their stupid secrecy."

Status effect: Unconscious. Time remaining: 3... 2... 1...

Jaxon's eyes opened. Once again, he had been forced out of the respawn room, and this time, he was slightly annoyed. He had been enjoying a Christmas movie and had just been getting to the part where the spoiled, city-girl, millionaire's daughter was about to kiss the sheepish small-town cowboy. Terrible timing.

"Here we are!" BackAttack had a dangerous gleam in his eyes. "In this bag you have enough food and water to last you a few days. There is *plenty* of light in there, so you don't need torches or anything like that. You can enter together or separately, but if you go in together, I hope you understand that the danger is twice as bad."

Jess and Jaxon locked eyes. Jaxon coughed into his hand before speaking, "Together?

"Sounds like a plan." Jess smiled at him.

"Aw. How cute." BackAttack shook his head. "Last chance to just leave will be right before you go past that big rock we are going to roll in to cover the entrance. If you turn around, we'll just kill you and hunt you both until we get bored, so feel free to do so."

Jaxon looked at the angry, young man quizzically. "You're a strange one."

"Just don't hate me, old man."

"Hmm. I must be giving off an 'old man' vibe again." Jaxon looked down the tunnel and took a few steps. "I don't hate you. A lot of people seem to think I have the time and energy for that. Nope. I either like you or don't think about you at all. Why would I give someone else power over me like that? Nah."

A few moments later, Jaxon's steps faltered. "Oh, I think I see why you are concerned about potential hatred."

Caution! You are about to enter the Dungeon of Occidendum. The only rewards that can be found in this dungeon are designed to assist in the murder of your own race, and therefore, there is a severe punishment for personal weakness. If you want to kill others so badly that you will risk this dungeon, please be aware that dying within this dungeon will result in character deletion. You cannot be forced into this dungeon. If you are placed inside against your will, you will automatically be transferred to a safe location.

"So if we fail here, we lose everything we've done the entire time we've been playing, huh?" Jaxon shrugged and looked at Jess. "Worth a shot, huh?"

Jess looked back, seeing ten daggers bared and pointing at her. "Looks like it is."

"You can always just let us kill you for a while!"

They ignored the Assassins and stepped into the dungeon together. The promised boulder was rolled into the entrance behind them, and Jess swallowed and pulled Jaxon into a hug. "Forward is the only way through, right?"

"Right."

"Thanks for risking everything for me, Jaxon." Jess teared up and looked into his smiling face. "I won't let you down."

"Don't worry; my team will get their money's worth out of you. I fully expect a discount on any services you can provide in the future." Jaxon patted her on the back as he walked past her and deeper into the tunnel.

"Ugh! Why do you *suck* so *much?*"

CHAPTER TWENTY-SEVEN

"So." Jaxon paused as the tunnel they were in started to widen into an actual room. It wouldn't be a good idea to just charge in without knowing what they were up against, especially not when that could mean a death with serious consequences. "Let's start practicing your craft. What do we do now?"

"What would you normally do?" Jess was sincerely curious, but to her disappointment, she got the exact answer she expected.

"I would go in and deal with whatever was waiting for me in there."

"Wrong answer and a good way to die." Jess sighed and shook her head. "The first step is going to be scouting. Going into an unknown area with unknown enemies leaves you ill-prepared and gives a large advantage to the defender. They will likely be in an environment that is specially prepared for them or their natural habitat if they are natural creatures."

"I'm picking up what you're laying down." Jaxon stared at her as she tried to figure out what he had just said. He sighed and rolled his eyes, which was disturbing due to the width at which they were always open. "Crystal clear, please continue?"

"Ah." Jess collected her thoughts and continued, "There are a few things we can assume right away: whatever is in here is going to be stronger than we are, at least individually. Also, there is some advantage to be had in stealth or else this player killer guild wouldn't have set up shop here. So my current plan is to act as our scout. I am going to go into this area as stealthily as possible, then come back and make a plan with you. Sound good?"

"Yes," Jaxon responded too loudly for Jess's comfort, and she glared at him before slinking away and into the room. Jaxon tried to be patient as the seconds turned into minutes... and the minutes began to tick by. He could see that she was unharmed thanks to having officially formed a party, but that didn't mean much to him at this point. While he was looking around, he noticed an inscription on the wall.

The wicked run when no one is chasing them.

Jaxon didn't see anything else and was starting to get bored. Just before deciding to go in after her, Jess arrived in the tunnel with him, panting and slightly scorched. She patted at her clothes, which were slightly smoking, took a deep breath, and sat down. "Alright, that sucked. Strange enemies in here. They look like gargoyles or at least what you expect to see on the top of old buildings, and they are *really* tough. They are either actual stone, or their bodies are just that hard. They can't seem to move their limbs very fast, so I don't think they are any good at physical fighting."

"Magical then?" Jaxon gestured at her smoldering shirt. "Some kind of spells?"

"In a way? I think it is more a spell-like ability." Jess considered for a moment but had nothing to add that could clarify. "It seems that wherever they look is flooded with heat. Not *fire* exactly but kind of like radiant heat from the sun. If they focus on something, that 'cone' of vision narrows over the course of a couple seconds and turns more into a laser or a beam of fire; to the point where it is actually visible and actual fire. But... compressed? As if it was solid. I *really* don't think being hit by that would be a good idea."

"Anything else?" Jaxon helped her to her feet, since it seemed that she had recovered.

"Yeah." She swallowed hard. "The effect stacks. Two of them saw me at the same time, and my shirt caught on fire; compared to when one saw me and I wasn't in danger until it's focus began to narrow. There are a bunch of them in this room, and the more that are looking at a particular thing, the hotter it gets. I'm betting that if a bunch of them focus enough on making a beam, they could disintegrate just about anything. I think we found why stealth works best through here."

"Well." Jaxon looked at the ground. "This could be an issue..."

"Yeah... I'm betting that they knew this area would likely kill you." Jess hesitated, trying to find anything encouraging. "At least they aren't stealthed?"

"I suppose." Jaxon leaned back and rolled his head a few times. "Welp, let's get going. You have a plan at all?"

"I do." Jess tried to sketch a plan in the air for Jaxon to follow, and he did his best. "This room is shaped like a giant crescent with no real cover at all. I think I should get across the area, make a bunch of noise, and get them all to look my way. Then you should go out and find a way to cross the room behind them. When they start looking at you, you need to find a way to use the others for cover. Alternatively, you could try to fight one while I distract the majority."

Jaxon sunk into thought, tapping at his chin and weaving around the room. He was walking in circles for a short while before Jess barked at him, "You are driving me *nuts*! There are only the two options! Pick one!"

"You said that there is a clear advantage to Rogues and stealthy types." Jaxon had an idea, an inkling that there was more to this place. "What do you think are the odds that BackAttack or the others defeated all the opponents when they came through here?"

"I'm... I guess *slim?*" Jess shook her head. "Jaxon, this is the first room. I highly doubt you want to take the time to fight everything in the dungeon, especially when the monsters are all this strong."

"I have an idea." Jaxon looked at her and let a smile bloom on his face that could have powered a third-world country. "Let's beat everything!"

Jess let her head fall back in exasperation, baring her neck as she stared at the sky. "Jaxon, *why?*"

"There has to be something *more* to this place," Jaxon stubbornly insisted. "We're going to find it. We are going to combine your ideas, though. If you can go get their attention, I'm going to start fighting the creature nearest me."

"Are you *sure* about this, Jaxon? You could end up being deleted," Jess softly reminded him.

"I have to do everything to the best of my abilities, Jess." Jaxon shooed her away, and she reluctantly went back into the room. "I'm not wicked; I won't run when I'm not being chased."

"I don't understand." Jess stared for a moment, but Jaxon shooed her away. It took about ten minutes, but Jaxon heard her voice echoing through the area, if faintly, "Rock for brains! Yeah, that's right, you overweight sloths! There ya go, over here!"

Jaxon peeked around the corner and saw that the nearest creature was ponderously turning in place to look the other direction. When it was facing away from him, he went into the crescent-room and walked over to inspect the armored being. Jaxon tapped at the creature, trying to find a weak point. The creature looked like a massive, ugly dog crossed with a dragon. It stood on four legs and had stubby wings on its back. It had no real neck, and so its head had a squashed appearance. Jaxon couldn't see its face, which was probably for the best.

Jaxon also noticed another fact when he looked around the room. It seemed that the light in the area was all generated by the creatures. At first, this hadn't been apparent, but as all the beasts finished turning toward Jess, the other side of the room became *very* dark. This only increased as their focus grew on Jess's location. The cone of light that each of them somehow projected began to narrow, not quite getting to the level Jess had spoken of but becoming more like a flashlight beam as they searched for the still-shouting woman.

Jaxon returned to tapping at the creature but wasn't finding any unarmored points. He was almost certain that the eyes would be a weak point, but the burning cone currently before them screamed 'bad idea to touch the eyes' to Jaxon. He decided to take a more direct route and punched the side of the dungeon mob.

-0

Alrighty, that didn't work at all. How about... *Adjust!*

-5

The creature let out a low, keening sound. Right away, the others in the room began shifting around, ignoring Jess's increasingly desperate shouting. Jaxon nodded and started punching the front leg of the beast. Zeros kept popping up in front of him, but by the time the creature had turned halfway around, Jaxon had been able to hit its knee forty times. He stepped back to see what would happen. "Adjust!"

-200

There was a mighty cracking, and the stiff knee of the strange thing shattered, causing it to slump forward and intensify its strange warning cry. The most important thing that happened was that Jaxon noticed that it could no longer look up at him very well. Its burning gaze had been mostly pointed at the floor but was also almost in contact with Jaxon's feet. He skipped around it and ran into the dark area of the room just as the first of the creatures began staring at the one that was crying out.

Perception +1. Wisdom +1.

The noisy beast was now the focus of all the others, and in moments, its exterior began melting away. Within twenty seconds, it had mostly melted to slag upon the floor. Jaxon thought 'mostly' for the simple reason that as the thing stopped being able to make noise, the others had looked away from it. On the plus side, he was now fairly certain that these were artificial constructs, as there had been no body beneath all of that stone.

*Exp: 85 (85 * Disappointed Defender x1).*

The statues were resetting, but Jess started to shout again. At first, there was no reaction, but then she ran over and hit one with the pommel of her dagger. It chimed, and the others started to move once more. Jaxon checked his stamina and debated attacking the next one as well. Activating adjust had used the forty-four stamina and had done far less damage than he had expected. He looked at the skill, cursing softly when he saw that the Master rank damage increase had vanished. The skill was back to doing only five points per stack, and he simply hadn't noticed in combat before now. Still, he could activate Adjust thirteen times in succession if he didn't need to use his stamina for anything else.

"Hey, Jess, ever heard the term 'staring a hole in something'? I think these are where that expression comes from," Jaxon called as he mimicked his previous tactic on the next Defender. She almost told him to keep it down but realized that the constructs were turning thanks to the alarm anyway. "They are pretty good experience, too! Eighty-five a pop."

"You *suck*!" Jess called back, irked that she hadn't gained any experience.

"Adjust!" Just as before, the leg of the creature broke. This time, Jaxon hadn't added enough stacks to break the leg off, so he decided to use forty hits as a baseline. It wouldn't do to be wasting stamina. He kicked the leg, again, and a third time. It broke off, and he barely got his foot out of the way as it fell forward. He ran over to another construct and began attacking it even as the others began melting down their fallen comrade. The one he was attacking began to call a warning, but the much louder one overrode whatever protocols these things had in place. Jaxon broke the leg off this one just as the other fell silent and found that he had gained a good battle rhythm.

It was slow, ponderous work, but he had finally defeated twenty-three of them and was working on the last. Jess came over to help out or possibly to steal experience. When Jaxon broke off the leg, he found another issue: there was no other creature to melt this one down. "Huh. How to do this..."

He started attacking the other front leg, taking nearly a minute to build up stacks. He stepped away and motioned for Jess to follow. "We might need to have a bit of distance. Also, I am nearly out of stamina."

Jaxon had needed to take a few breaks throughout this process, but he was hoping this would be worth doing. With a thought, the construct's leg shattered fully and caused large cracks to appear where it had been connected.

-800.

"Whew." Jaxon watched as the Defender fell forward and had its face pressed against the ground. Jess looked at him and started to say something, but he waved her off and pointed. Sure enough, after a few seconds, the ground began to bubble and melt. Jess and Jaxon left the room and walked through the hallway, getting a notification a minute later that the final construct had been destroyed. Then they got the notification Jaxon had been hoping for.

Exp: 1,955 (85 * Disappointed Defender x23).

You have cleared the first layer of the Dungeon of Occidendum. These must be cleared in order, else only a standard reward will be given. Layers cleared 1/4.

"I knew it!" Jaxon turned and grabbed Jess. "We can *complete* this dungeon. We don't have to just *survive* it!"

CHAPTER TWENTY-EIGHT

There was apparently a reason that the notification had told them the layers needed to be cleared in a particular order. When Jess came back from the next scouting mission, she was happy to inform Jaxon that the next enemy had living, fleshy opponents that could be killed fairly easily. She thought that they were likely easy prey for BackAttack or really any Assassin that came through here.

Jaxon had studied the walls as they walked, and found another small inscription that read: '*Don't let shame control you.*'

He decided that this phrase meant that it was time for a head-on fight, and it looked like the creatures in here didn't have any weapons, armor, or magical effects surrounding them. Jaxon confidently walked out and punched one of them in the face, and when the others started coming toward him, he activated Living Weapons and started to tear into them. Lefty and Terror were *very* effective against this type of enemy and were happily tearing chunks out of the humanoids.

Jaxon was now in the middle of a group of them, already standing over a few bodies. He swung at the nearest one and received a shock—literally—just before his T-Rex hand would have impacted. There was a slight distortion in the air, and it seemed to be surrounding Jaxon on all sides. No... it was actually coming from the creatures, seemingly connecting all of them as they turned to face him. They didn't attack, simply staring at him and shaking their heads. More of the monstrous humanoids started joining into the circle, and all of them slowly started shaking their heads back and forth. As more arrived, the distortion became more solidified.

Jaxon glanced at his notifications while allowing his hands to eat away at the fallen bodies. He needed to be ready for a fight, and they were able to recover Mana from eating. So... win-win.

*Exp: 279 (31 * Circle of Shame Member x9).*

"I seem to be trapped in a circle of shame!" Jaxon called out, his words echoing slightly. "The enemies in this place seem to be designed to convey how poorly the general population thinks of killing members of your own race, but they also create an electric barrier if they surround you!"

As he finished speaking, the members took a step forward, and the energetic circle moved toward him. After they moved, the circle became more transparent but quickly solidified once again. "I think they are going to close in on me and shock me to death! I would like to be rescued, please! I can be the damsel in distress. I really don't mind! Frankly, I'm always surprised that that trope is always thought so poorly of. From where I'm standing, the idea of rescue is *very* appealing!"

The circle closed in once more, and Jaxon took a nasty shock before crouching down. A few seconds later, just as he expected the walls to close in for the final time, Jess slew three of the members in quick succession as they stepped forward. Jaxon dove through the break in the circle before the members could close around him once more and, with Jess's help, quickly finished off the rest of the monsters.

*Exp: 651 (31 * Circle of Shame Member x21).*

Jaxon looked over at Jess and batted his eyelashes. "My *hero!*"

"I could hear you, Jaxon." Jess rolled her eyes as Jaxon clasped his hands together and pretended to swoon. "Oh, *stop* that!"

You have cleared a layer of the Dungeon of Occidendum. Layers cleared 2/4.

"But back to something you said earlier, yes, I think this place is designed to inform you that you will be looked down upon by not only the game but other people when you kill another of your race simply to improve your own lot in life." Jess sighed and slapped Jaxon on the arm. "Thanks for rescuing me from the guild."

"Eh, we'll see about that. I'm happy that we are giving it a try, though." Jaxon waved off her concerns as they moved to the next layer. Again, Jess went and scouted ahead, this time coming back with a scowl on her face. "Just a few monsters but big and powerful. They are also carrying weapons that are bigger than I am."

"How many in total?" Jaxon questioned her while looking for a phrase on the wall.

"Three."

"Alright. Do you want to be the attacker or the bait?" Jaxon's words caused her to sputter, and she refused to meet his eye. "Got it, you want to be the attacker."

She nodded sharply, and he continued, "Good. If they are weapon users, I think I learned my lesson from the Lemure. I'm pretty sure I can handle this if we work fast. Let me know when you are ready."

Jaxon found the phrase and took his time to carefully consider the extra-cryptic message. *'You can elude the Law, but if it catches you, prepare to be broken.'*

Just to be on the safe side, they waited until they had recovered all of their energy and Jaxon's Living Weapons had come off of cooldown before entering the room. Jaxon saw the enemies right away, since it was hard to miss them. They were at least eight feet tall and were carrying melee weapons: a sword, a hammer, and a truncheon respectively. The most off-putting feature was the fact that their arms were at least twice as long as the creatures were tall, though otherwise they could have easily been called simple Giants. They seemed to be expecting Jaxon and nodded at him as they got into position.

Jaxon nodded back. After all, there was no need to be impolite, even if you were entering a deathmatch. Jess had come into the room before him and was slinking around the side, hugging the wall. It was easy to see that these large enemies could be snuck past; in fact, Jaxon would have tried it himself if he wasn't following in Joe's footsteps as a completionist. This might be the only chance he ever had to attempt this dungeon, so he needed to make the most of it.

Jaxon came into range, and without a word escaping their lips, the Giants attacked. Jaxon rolled forward under a hammer that had twenty-two feet of wind-up behind it. With the strength of a Giant and the power of momentum, when the hammer struck, it not only caused a crater, it formed a shockwave that carried a surprised Jaxon through the air and just *barely* over a sword that was sweeping across the ground. Obviously, these beings were well practiced in working together, and only sheer, dumb luck had saved Jaxon from his overly obvious method of dodging.

Luck +1.

Really lucky then. It was obvious that he wouldn't have survived that slice. Jaxon threw himself to the side, assuming that a truncheon or hammer would be following him. He only managed to look paranoid, since the last of the Giants was currently gripping its pelvic region with a look of mixed pain and horror. A meaty splat echoed through the room just before the Giant shrieked.

"It was the only place I could reach in time!" Jess called to a shaken Jaxon. That Giant sunk to its knees, whimpering as the remaining Giants and Jaxon shared a wincing glance. Seeing that he was being genuinely disturbed, the Giants didn't fly into a rage; but it was obvious that they were taking this battle far more seriously now.

Once more the hammer came down, but this time, it was *way* faster. The Giant was using both hands and focusing evenly on his target. Jaxon rolled backward, springing up and forward just before impact. He landed on the outstretched arm and started running toward the Giant's main body.

"Jess! Look! I'm an *anime!*" Jaxon shouted as he activated Living Weapons and prepared to jump at an unprotected face. A small dagger sunk into his foot just before he leapt, pinning him to the arm below. "*Ah!*"

A wall of steel dropped inches from his nose, moving so fast that Jaxon could barely see it. His position shifted, and the arm he was pinned to along with the other that was gripping the hammer fell to the ground. The now-armless Giant was staring at his comrade in shock, blood spurting from the stumps of his biceps. The sword-wielding Giant looked surprised and speechless; and since he stood there frozen, he was an easy target for Jess to finish off by plunging her daggers into each of his eyes. Jaxon took the time to kill the armless Giant, and then Jess put the still-whimpering one out of his misery.

Exp: 900 (300 * Long Arm Of The Law x3).

You have cleared a layer of the Dungeon of Occidendum. Layers cleared 3/4.

"By the way," Jess panted as she stood upright and brushed her hair out of her eyes, "you can't be 'an anime'. At best you would be an anime *character.*"

Jaxon attempted to retaliate, "At best *you* can... you can... please don't chop off any more penises."

Jess choked back a gasping laugh and started coughing. "I *really* wasn't going for that, but... yeah. Plus, the plural of the word is *penii*."

"So long as you don't do it again, I don't care *what* you call it." Jaxon firmly informed her. To his chagrin, she only shrugged.

"Hey. No promises. It's a weak point and a surefire critical hit."

Jaxon paused, then shook his head. "Oh. I guess I really don't care about that fact. At all."

CHAPTER TWENTY-NINE

"It's the *final layer!*" Jaxon stated as they walked down an incline.

"If you burst into song, I'm going to do to *you* what I did to that *Giant*," Jess growled, her words making Jaxon choke as he did his best to not say *anything* that could be considered lyrical. "Hey! Whoa! I did it! I finally got the Intimidation skill! I've been trying to get that since I started the game!"

"Aw, you didn't need it!" Jaxon reached over for a hug that she dodged. "You made friends even without the skill!"

"That's *exactly what the skill is used for*," Jess informed him with a concerned glance.

"Right, that's why I said it."

"What?"

"What, what?" They had a tiny staring contest, but Jaxon's constant shifting and wiggling made him win easily. "So, gonna scout this one out as well? Seriously, I could just call you Scout and people would eventually know who I was talking about."

"No comments from the peanut gallery, please." Jess crept into the room, coming back moments later. "Big room, one opponent, looks like a lady. She has a harp but no other discernible weapons. I'm guessing she's a Boss of some sort. There is a treasure chest on the other side of the room, but since we are trying to clear this place, I say we sneak attack the witch."

Jess entered the room *well* ahead of Jaxon so that she could get into position for a sneak attack. Jaxon waited until three minutes had passed, then stepped boldly into the room. He didn't expect the Boss to speak or for it to have such a *beautiful* voice. "Finally, a visitor!"

Jaxon shook off his surprise and slowly closed his fists. "I'm sorry, but I am not here to visit. I'm here to clear this dungeon."

"Ah. How *tragic*." The lady clasped her hands over her heart and looked like she was about to burst into tears. She grabbed her harp and strummed a few notes. "Why do you want to kill your own people so badly? No, don't answer. Before you kill them, before you try to kill *me*, you must defeat... *yourself*."

She played a powerful chord, and a pale imitation of Jaxon began to appear. "Most people can't understand what it truly means to win against your best self, to *become* your best self—*ack*!"

Jess had arrived behind the woman and was stabbing her repeatedly. "*No*! That is *such* an overused concept. I *refuse* to be subjected to such a crappy, stupid, overdone, repetitive, *trope*!"

The woman struggled and made a few wet noises, but the knives slamming into her made it impossible for her to say anything or cast other spells. She fell to the ground, and the misty Jaxon vanished. Jess kicked the woman once more for good measure and looked over at Jaxon. "We did it!"

"Ah... yeah!" Jaxon lightly laughed. He was barely nervous at *all*.

Exp: 500 (500 * Self-Obsessed Siren x1).

You have cleared a layer of the Dungeon of Occidendum. Layers cleared 4/4. You have cleared the Dungeon of Occidendum! As the first people to ever clear the dungeon, you will be given the standard dagger reward, a reward based on your class, and gain the ability to select a new goal for the dungeon. You have been granted a title!

Title gained: Stand Defiant. You have overcome an area meant to destroy you and have gained the tools needed to

*destroy others. Whether you intend to stand for humanity... or
against it... you will be prepared. +20% damage done to humans.
-10% damage taken from humans.*

They popped open the treasure chest and grabbed the
multiple items that appeared in it.

*Item Gained: Graverobber's Kris (Rare). Killing a
member of your race with this weapon will allow you to loot
their body. More benefits may be found over time.*

*Item Gained: Dino Treat (Unique) (Class Item). This is
the favored treat of carnivorous dinosaurs everywhere! Useful for
taming the majestic creatures. Using this item on any form of
dinosaur will permanently increase their disposition toward you
by a full rank! Only use it once per day for the effect to take
hold! Uses: 2/2.*

*You have taken control of a Perma-death dungeon! As
the new dungeon keepers, you may choose a new option for the
dungeon's growth. Leaving it 'as is' will grant you 10% of all
experience lost by those who die in the dungeon. Changing the
goal will reset the dungeon and remove your roles as the
dungeon keepers.*

"This... this might be the single greatest reward I've
ever gotten from a quest or test." Jess was staring at the screen
longingly. "Can we just leave it as is? No one else knows that
you can capture it, and we could gain experience from this for
years!"

"At the cost of a person losing their character every
single time we get a reward," Jaxon reminded her instantly.

She grimaced and groaned. "Oh, come *on*! The people
that come in here are all going to be *bad* people anyway!"

" *We* are in here right now." Jaxon's words made her
sigh. "How about we just look at the options?"

"Fine," she replied shortly, and a window appeared in front of them.

Options for the dungeon:

As Is (Player Vs Player): Allow the dungeon to continue giving rewards specialized in hunting people of the same race as the user. (You will gain 10% of the experience lost by any person who falls in the dungeon).

Player Vs Environment: Allow the dungeon to give rewards specialized in hunting non-sentient creatures.

Environmental Bully: Allow the dungeon to give rewards specialized in hunting non-sentient creatures weaker than the user.

Player Defense: Allow the dungeon to give rewards specialized in protecting members of the user's race.

Player Growth: Allow the dungeon to give rewards specialized in boosting the stats of the user to the maximum, including scaling weapons.

"Well, I'd say player growth for sure." Jess's eyes were shining at the thought of super-powered weapons helping her travel through the game with ease.

"One *small* thing you're forgetting." Jaxon grimaced and poked her in the forehead. "We. Don't. Get. To. Come. Back. Whatever we choose now is only going to benefit the killers out there."

Wisdom +1.

"Ah, dang." Jess rubbed her head and glared at the options. "Let's go total opposite again. Player defense looks like it would either force this guild out of a job, or it would make them shift their focus to something actually productive."

"I think that'd be the best option," Jaxon agreed solemnly. "Let's do it! I want to give my Dino's a treat! Let's do it, go, go, go!"

Player 'Jessamyn' has selected the option 'Player Defense'. Do you agree to convert the dungeon's mission to this option? Yes / No.

"Yes!" Jaxon cheerfully stated. The window vanished, only to be replaced by another.

Once you leave the dungeon, it will be locked for 24 hours as needed changes are made.

"Oh, good. That'll give us some time to escape." Jaxon tapped his fingers along his arm, thinking about their next move. "We both have the dagger? Alright, let me feed my hands real quick."

He opened this box of Dino Treats and pulled out what looked like a brick of bloody meat and fat that had been compressed to become as solid as possible. Activating Living Weapons, he made sure to start with the T-Rex heads pointing at him.

"Craw?"

"Nyah?"

"Lefty, Terror, you've been *very* good in here. *Good* T-Rex Head Hands. *Good!*" After speaking, he turned his arms and let them see the thick brick of... stuff. As soon as they saw the treat, both of them let out a triumphant roar and fought to get closer to it. Jaxon didn't fight back, and soon, his hands were fighting over the scraps. The treat had luckily refilled his Mana as they ate, or they wouldn't even have gotten halfway through the dense rectangle.

When they had finished, the hands turned back toward Jaxon with interest. "Cra~a~aw?"

"That's all for now, Terror."

"Nyah!"

"You too, Lefty. *Good* work today!" As he finished speaking, his Mana petered out, and his hands returned to normal.

Your Living Weapons' disposition has shifted from 'Confused' to 'Timid'. They are now 30% less likely to attack you if they come in range! Dino Treat can be used again in 23:59.

"So, I need to know..." Jess looked over at the shimmering portal that had appeared in midair. "How are you planning to deal with the people that are almost *assuredly* waiting for us out there?"

"I *do* have a plan. Are you ready for this?"

"From the look you're giving me... probably not."

CHAPTER THIRTY

"You made it." BackAttack stared at the duo as they walked out of the dungeon and into a large, stone warehouse.

"No need to sound so happy about it," Jess spat back bitterly. She had to pretend that she was upset about the outcome of their deal, or everything would be for naught.

BackAttack shrugged. "It was a giant waste of my time, but so long as you have my daggers, it *might* have been worth it. Hand them over, and we'll send you on your way."

"The way you phrase that sure sounds like it'll end well for us." Jess narrowed her eyes at the Guild Leader.

"Well, Jess, I can't have you learning the location of our secret headquarters, now can I?" The Assassin actually cracked a smile at that. "Hand over the daggers."

Jaxon cleared his throat and took a confident step forward. "Ah, *actually*, the deal was that we would give you *a* dagger, if you recall correctly."

"No, the deal was for *two* daggers." BackAttack gripped his daggers and seemed to be on the verge of using them.

"Nope. We had just *talked* about two daggers. Then for the deal, I only said *a* dagger." Jaxon put his newly acquired dagger on the ground and slid it over. "Go ahead and pick that up."

BackAttack slowly bent over and grabbed the dagger. As he did, a notification appeared in front of the two of them.

Obligation fulfilled! 'Jaxon' has honored his end of the deal made between him and 'BackAttack'. So long as he does not discuss the daggers with others after this point, this deal is intact.

"You conniving little..." BackAttack snarled, having to physically hold himself back from slaying the two of them. Then, abruptly, his expression changed. "Fine then, fair enough. I suppose my part of the deal only says that *I* won't hunt or kill you, doesn't it? I'll just have to have my guild take you out whenever I want."

"And *that* is why we would like to give you this other dagger in return for a small addendum to our deal." Jaxon blithely smiled. "We hand this over, you don't send people after us either intentionally or by negligence. I realized that we had both made a small error when setting up the deal, you see."

"As soon as you are off my territory, agreed," BackAttack quickly stated, walking over and grabbing the Kris after a small notification told them the details of their new deal. "I hope to never see you again, freak."

"The feeling is mutual, but I'm *sure* we'll cross paths eventually."

BackAttack turned and walked to the exit, pausing just before he stepped through. "I'm not hunting you right now; you are just *in my territory*. Boys, send them to respawn and loot the bodies."

"*Booo!*" Jaxon called after the shadowy figure, his hands cupped around his mouth. BackAttack looked back only once with a smirk on his face before vanishing entirely.

Jess shifted so that she was standing back-to-back with Jaxon, and a shimmering dagger appeared in her main hand. In the other, she still held the bone dagger given by the Wolfmen. "Are you sure about this?"

"It's working out exactly as we predicted, isn't it?" Jaxon smiled at the figures around them winningly, even though they were beginning to fade from sight. "Before we fight, how about a bet?"

Only one person was still visible, the man who had found them at the bar and drugged them. He smiled right back at Jaxon, his head cocked to the side. "*Oh*? What would we want from you that we can't just... *take*?"

"Well now, let me see." Jaxon pretended to be thinking deeply. He snapped his fingers and met the eyes of the man in front of him. "Ah! I know! One of the functions of those nasty daggers is that only one item can be looted, and it is seemingly random, yes? Well, you see that *extra* shiny dagger Jess is carrying? See how beyond that she has only basic gear and is only *carrying* basic gear? I'll wager that shiny dagger."

"What if we just want to take our chances?" The man's eyes were dancing in amusement, no doubt because the others were closing in around the duo.

"*Your* potential loss." Jaxon shrugged nonchalantly. "In return, all I'm asking for if we win is a five-minute head start. No attacking us for five minutes! If we escape the territory you own, all the better. I'm pretty sure you will be killing us either way if you win."

"I suppose I can agree to that, but what is it that we are wagering *on*?" The happy Assassin motioned for his people to wait.

"I want you to pick your strongest person, and we will determine the winner on a single match." Jaxon smiled darkly, even though his teeth glimmered in the light. "An *arm-wrestling* match. I win, we don't get attacked for five minutes by anyone who knows about the deal. My opponent wins, we hand over the dagger."

"Arm wrestling. How very 'high-school' of you." The Assassin shook his head and looked at the others. "You're a strange one, alright. Guys, you all good with this? ...Looks like we have a deal."

A notification appeared and was waved away. There must have been some kind of signal because one of the men appeared in front of Jaxon while others brought over a small table and two chairs. Jaxon looked over the brute of a man that sat down, wincing as the Assassin who was oddly and obviously disposed toward the strength stat got ready. Jaxon sat down and glanced at Jess. "Get ready to run. As soon as I win this, we go straight through the door and don't stop until we find a safe location."

Jess nodded even as the ogre of a man sitting across from him scoffed and placed his elbow on the table. "Let's do this, tiny."

Jaxon placed his hand in the other man's palm and waited for the happy Assassin to start the countdown. "Alright, boys! Three... two... one... go!"

Jaxon activated Living Weapons just before the man said 'go', his hands shifting into T-Rex Heads that tore into the meaty hand holding them. Jaxon made sure to slam the Brute's hand into the table, ensuring his victory. In fact, a notification appeared to that effect. As the huge man screamed, Jaxon looked around at the shocked faces of the Assassins. "Looks like I get five minutes of you not fighting me."

He slammed Lefty into his opponent's neck and tore it out with a wet splash of blood. Then he twisted to the side and cartwheeled over the previously-happy Assassin and sunk his hand's teeth into his thigh as he tried to get some distance. On the other side of the room, Jess was stabbing everyone around her. They drew their weapons and tried to join combat, but the view of anyone attempting to do so was blocked for a crucial second by a notification warning them that they would gain the Warlock title if they did so.

During that moment of hesitation, Jess slew the people around her in an acrobatic display of violence. Jaxon had torn large chunks of meat out of his target's legs and moved on to anyone else he could find that wasn't already incapacitated. He left all of his targets alive, though they would need to go to respawn or find a powerful healer if they wanted to walk again.

Jaxon was standing near a crate, and let his hands drift around the corner. He stage whispered, "*Don't move!* My hands can't see you if you *don't move!*"

"Wha?" The confused voice attracted Lefty's attention, and the T-Rex head clamped onto the Assassin that had accidentally broken stealth. Jaxon tore off a chunk of meat and looked back at the room.

"That's enough. Let's go!" Jaxon demanded, cartwheeling over to the door and pulling it open. Jess ran through, and they started running down the hallways looking for the exits. Jaxon looked at Jess, noticing that she had a deep red color suffusing her name, as well as a visibly red aura around her. Drat, she had gained the player killer's aura for attacking first. Jaxon had a lighter red aura, but the only man he had killed had *technically* been in combat and grappling him at the time; his aura came from *attacking* other players.

Either way, they would need to do their best to avoid others for a few days while the auras faded away. Luckily, they had a couple days of travel ahead of them if they wanted to get back to the Wanderer's Guild base. On the third try, the two of them found an exit and got outside, running into the woods as the alarm was raised behind them.

They would be chased to the edge of what this guild considered their territory, and they were fine with that. The hunt was on, but luckily Jess and Jaxon had become quite experienced in remaining awake for long periods of time while running through a forest.

EPILOGUE

Two people appeared in Jay's view. Once again, he had been assigned punishment guard duty and was guarding the only wall around the scoured village. He tightened his grip on his spear as he saw that one of the people coming toward him had a player killer aura, but it winked out in moments, making him doubt what he had just been seeing. Then he looked at the other person and went pale.

"Is that *Jay*?" Jaxon ran over to the guard, who was holding his spear level albeit shakily. A moment later, Jess had caught up to the skipping Jaxon, but Jay was already laying on the ground groaning from a sudden, brutal adjustment. "You're welcome, Jay! See you next time, good buddy!"

"What did you just do to him?" Jess asked as they walked through the small gate.

"Standing adjustment." Jaxon looked over happily. "He asked me for a recurring treatment plan and started a tab. Nothing like being well-known enough that people become returning customers!"

"*You!*" Jess turned toward the shout, noticing a pompous looking young man surrounded by guards walking toward them. "You were *banished* you filthy–"

"Jaxon! There you are!" another voice cut into the mix, and Jess looked over to see a bald man wearing robes striding toward them with a happy smile. He also had people with him, but these seemed more... varied. There was a stout man with a pair of axes, a raven-haired lady with pale skin and deep bags under her eyes, and a colorfully dressed man wearing a ridiculous hat. "Everyone just got back a short while ago. I was hoping that we could get up to date on our adventures. What do you think?"

"*Excuse* me. Get *out* of the way." The pompous man seemed to be nearly hyperventilating over the interruption, his fists clenched and pale. "We told you what would happen if you came back, and you are–"

The bald man stepped up to Jaxon, still chatting happily, and the pompous youth seemed absolutely shocked that he had done so. "Are you not in the Guild? I *said*, get out of the *way!*"

"Right, *that's* enough of *that.* I'm *Joe.* Who are you?" The bald man, Joe, turned to the other and seemed to become... different. Darker, dangerous... deadly. A powerful aura of magic stifled those around him, an actual physical pressure that made it hard to breathe.

"I...I'm–"

"I don't actually care. Leave us alone." Joe turned back to Jaxon, suddenly all smiles again. "Jaxon, what happened to you? What are you *wearing?*"

"Oh, it's been an interesting few days!" Jaxon cheerfully stated, giving Joe an unwanted hug that left a thin film of blood and sweat on Joe's clothes. The bald man gave a weak smile and made a hand motion. A disk of water traveled up and down their bodies, followed by Jess's as an afterthought. She felt cleaner than she had in a week after it passed over her. "Ah, I've missed your tricks. Oh! Before I go too far, I need to feed my hands a treat. Been too busy the last few days to really do so."

"Feed yer... hands?" One of the men standing next to Joe smiled uncomfortably. "Ah feel like ya have an interesting story fer me ta tell."

"One... moment." Jaxon ignored the others, including the pompous man's group who was still standing awkwardly near them. A box appeared in Jaxon's hands, from which he pulled a brick of meat. With a strange distortion, Jaxon's hands shifted and began tearing into the meat.

The people in the area all shouted, flinched, or took a step backward, with two notable exceptions: Jess, as she was used to this, and Joe, who took a step closer with wonder filling his eyes. As the Living Weapons finished their snack, Jaxon held them aloft so they could roar their joy into the sky.

"Are those...?"

"T-Rex Head Hands," Jaxon cheerfully stated, pulling the now-placid creatures closer to his body. "They are a skill called Living Weapons."

"T-Rex... Head... Hands." Joe's eyes were burning with excitement, and as the other group took the chance to escape the situation, Joe looked like he wanted nothing more than to grab the miniature beasts and study them. "Long name. If they always come out together, could we call them something else?"

Jaxon smiled happily. Now *here* was a man who appreciated the finer things in life. "Sure, Joe. What did you have in mind?"

"How about 'Rexus'?"

"Interesting. Rexus." Jaxon rolled the word around in his mouth for a moment. "Rex, as in King, which is where T-Rex comes from in the first place. Rexus as a whole, though... that means 'a mature, self-possessed, and responsible nature'. Absolutely *flawless*, Joe. That describes me perfectly."

AFTERWORD

Thank you for reading! I hope you enjoyed Rexus! Since reviews are the lifeblood of indie publishing, I'd love it if you could leave a positive review on Amazon! Please use this link to go to the Completionist Chronicles: Rexus Amazon product page: geni.us/Rexus.

As always, thank you for your support! You are the reason I'm able to bring these stories to life.

ABOUT DAKOTA KROUT

I live in a 'pretty much Canada' Minnesota city with my wife and daughter. I started writing The Divine Dungeon series because I enjoy reading and wanted to create a world all my own. To my surprise and great pleasure, I found like-minded people who enjoy the contents of my mind. Publishing my stories has been an incredible blessing thus far and I hope to keep you entertained for years to come!

Connect with Dakota:
Patreon.com/DakotaKrout
Facebook.com/TheDivineDungeon

ABOUT MOUNTAINDALE PRESS

Dakota and Danielle Krout, a husband and wife team, strive to create as well as publish excellent fantasy and science fiction novels. Self-publishing *The Divine Dungeon: Dungeon Born* in 2016 transformed their careers from Dakota's military and programming background and Danielle's Ph.D. in pharmacology to President and CEO, respectively, of a small press. Their goal is to share their success with other authors and provide captivating fiction to readers with the purpose of solidifying Mountaindale Press as the place 'Where Fantasy Transforms Reality.'

Connect with Mountaindale Press:
MountaindalePress.com
Facebook.com/MountaindalePress
Krout@MountaindalePress.com

Mountaindale Press Titles

GameLit and LitRPG

The Divine Dungeon Series
The Completionist Chronicles Series
By: Dakota Krout

A Touch of Power: Siphon
By: Jay Boyce

Red Mage: Advent
By: Xander Boyce

Peaks of Power: Beginnings
By: Paul Campbell Jr.

Pixel Dust: Party Hard
By: David Petrie

Coming soon!

Ether Collapse: Equalize
By: Ryan DeBruyn

Axe Druid: Into the Light
By: Christopher Johns

Skeleton in Space: Histaff
By: Andries Louws

FANTASY

Coming soon!

The Lost Sigil: Insurrection
By: RAYMOND BECKHAM and DARIUS COOK

The Black Knight Trilogy
By: CHRISTIAN J. GILLILAND

Appendix

Notable Characters

Alexis – Joe's second-in-command for his current team, Alexis is an Aromatic Artificer. By making poisons and weapons and using them to great effect, she has proven her worth time and again.

Aten – The Commander of 'The Wanderer's' Noble Guild.

BackAttack Beastbane – An Assassin who runs a high-powered player killer's guild. Very mysterious.

Bard – Bard holds the position of a tank in Joe's current team. Contrary to his name,
Bard is a Skald. Instead of staying in a well-protected position and playing songs, Bard is on the frontlines of any engagement chanting and swinging his axes.

CAL – Certified Altruistic Lexicon, the AI that controls Eternium.

Jaxon – An acupuncturist and chiropractor in real life, Jaxon came into the game to try out new methods of healing. Is it his fault that everyone is so... brittle? Playing the game as a Monk, Jaxon uses his talents to deadly effect.

Jessamyn – Having joined Eternium in hopes of gaining a spot on a guild specializing in player killing, the wannabe-assassin has her hopes dashed by Jaxon. Her attitude shifts as she realizes that Jaxon has a better place for her to go.

Joe – The main character of our story, Joe is a Ritualist who has specialized into a 'Rituarchitect' class. By supplying the material and power, he can grow a building with ease. His contributions in the future will need to be significant for the human race to survive...

Poppy – Papadopoulos Whisperfoot is a Duelist who wears eye-catching clothes and wields a rapier. Able to take down heavily-armored foes with ease, Poppy is an invaluable member of Joe's current team.

Jaxon's Final Stats

Name: Jaxon 'Legend' Class: **Bonecruncher**
Profession: Chiropractor
Bonecruncher Level: 1 Exp: 0 Exp to next level: 1,000
Level: 12 Exp: 81,621 Exp to next level: 9,379
Hit Points: 455/455 (50+(400)+5) (Base 50 plus 10 points for each point in Constitution, once it has increased above 10.)
Mana: 350/350 (12.5 mana per point of Intelligence.)
Mana regen: 9.75 (Wisdom multiplied by .25 mana regen per second)

Stamina: 575/575 (50+(315)+(190)) (Base 50 plus 5 points for each point in strength and constitution, once each of the stats has increased above 10.)

Characteristic: Raw score (Modifier)

Strength: 75 (2.25)
Dexterity: 102 (3.02)
Constitution: 50 (2.0)
Intelligence: 28 (1.28)
Wisdom: 39 (1.39)
Charisma: 6 (0.06)
Perception: 24 (1.24)
Luck: 48 (1.48)
Karmic Luck: 0